When I first stepped in through the sturdy, oak doors to the mansion, I caught a great waft of, I don't know how else to put it, an *exotic* smell.

Maybe it's the smell of cool draughts over marble floors. Or the cinnamon scents that seemed to have been smudged into just about every material, every pillow, every bed sheet, the covers of the sofas, and the curtains.

Perhaps it's just the feeling of having got away.

Because, truly, I couldn't be happier.

Beating sun. Blue skies. Fresh lime juice.

What could possibly go wrong?

Snarky, ill-tempered and alone:
Anna Harris kills for money.

Weightier paycheques. Bigger risks. Longer bills.
She can see no way of turning work down.

She heads for Spain.

Beating sun. Blue skies. Fresh lime juice.

What could possibly go wrong?

A twisting, turning story which proves that you can run
from your problems but they will always find you.

KILLER PUBLICITY

BLOOD SPORTS

THE SECOND MATHEWSON MEDIA NOVEL

- AV IAIN -

Blood Sports: The Second Mathewson Media Novel

ISBN-10: 1-78532-009-2

ISBN-13: 978-1-78532-009-5

Published by DIB Books, 2014.
www.dibbooks.com

THE ANNA HARRIS SERIES

Novels

Good Press
Blood Sports
Kill Switch
Hell Bird
Death Log

Collections

Dressed To Kill

BLOOD SPORTS

THE SECOND MATHEWSON MEDIA NOVEL

- AV IAIN -

CHAPTER ONE

So Brian gave me time off. How nice of him. I guess that's the best he could do after spending the last few months manipulating me all that he could—bending me to just about his every whim for the power games he was playing.

I'm not bitter, though. Oh no, Anna Harris bitter, never on your life.

How can I be bitter with this view?

Rolling yellow-green hills for miles around. Pale orange dust rising up gently in the warm, slightly stilted breeze. And the gentle hum of insects in the tall grasses, all around.

Maybe later on tonight those insects'll *gently* drive me berserk. But, for now, the novelty's still in. Hey, I just got here.

And I can just about see the sea on the horizon, a marble-blue glow, almost not quite there, but it is. And I'm almost certain I can smell the salt carrying on the wind, that distinct *sea* smell.

Spain.

Don't really know why I said 'Spain' when Brian asked me where I wanted to go. *Anywhere* in the world I wanted to go and think over my career, think if this *killing* was really what I wanted to do with my life. If I really want to go on killing for Brian.

But I said Spain to him, and I can't say that I'm regretting my decision. At least not thus far.

Some bulked-up guy with green-tinted glasses, a black suit and a thatch of blond hair met me at the airport. He spoke no English. Come to think of it, he didn't speak at all. But he drove me over here, along these sand-dusted roads, and up to this . . . well, there's really no other way of putting it . . . to this *mansion*.

I wonder if Brian has a house in every country on the face of the Earth. That really wouldn't surprise me all that much. If I'd said Turkey, or Bahrain, or Belize, would he have had a mansion there, and a blond, suited-up guy all waiting to drive me?

One thing's for certain, while I'm out here, while I'm *on holiday*, there's no chance I'm going to give Brian a ring. Not even going to check my email. And it's not just me insisting on it. Brian stated that if I so much as called him to ask how to turn up the temperature of the pool, he would have an especially lethal Spanish assassin despatched post-haste to, well, *despatch* of me.

And though he said it as a bit of a joke, I have to admit it sent a little bit of a shudder up my spine. And that overwhelming minty flavour that seems to stick around Mathewson Media—Brian's public image company, and, I suppose, my *direct* employer—got the better of me. Sent me a little nauseous.

But the mansion. Wow. All white. Of course it is. Anything else would've been *extravagant*.

It reminds me of when I went to visit a museum, I don't remember its name, or particularly when, but it was just like this, with great big stone pillars with spiral designs running up them, and that same slicked-on coat of white paint, of course.

The museum had the same sturdy, stone steps leading up to it too.

That's probably where the similarities end, though, because, most likely, that museum I went to visit didn't have sprawling verdant gardens springing up all over—that surely take a good deal of watering all year round—or an enormous swimming pool outback with a beach-style, bamboo-roofed bar parked beside it.

The funny thing about this place is that it feels a little lonely. I did think about bringing my cat, Lizzie, but thought better of it. Not really wanting to test her out on a plane.

So she's staying with Arnold and the kids.

Guess that makes Kate feel pretty lucky considering that she's allergic.

When I first stepped in through the sturdy, oak doors to the mansion, I caught a great waft of, I don't know how else to put it, an *exotic* smell.

Maybe it's the smell of cool draughts over marble floors. Or the cinnamon scents that seemed to have been smudged into just about every material, every pillow, every bed sheet, the covers of the sofas, and the curtains.

Perhaps it's just the feeling of having got away.

Because, truly, I couldn't be happier.

Beating sun. Blue skies. Fresh lime juice.

What could possibly go wrong?

I pick out the master bedroom to dump my suitcase, because I reckon that if I'm going to do this at all, then I'd be best off doing this *properly*. And Brian didn't say anything about which bedroom I should pick out in the mansion, or if there was anything I should try and go out of my way not to break.

Like I said before, he probably has so many mansions scattered about the world that he has a hard time keeping track of the minutiae of every one.

I know that I would.

Just like the rest of the mansion, the master bedroom is done out in white. White everywhere.

From the bed sheets, to the bath towels, to the netted curtains.

I stride up to the netted curtains, part them to one side, and then realise there's a balcony.

That's the thing with mansions, or what I've seen of my handful of them, they're constantly full of surprises.

I step out onto the balcony, seize hold of the brass railings. They're cool, though there's no reason why they shouldn't be, and the balcony gives a view out across the sandy plains, and gives that bluish glimmer of sea right there on the horizon.

I love to be beside the sea. I can think of nothing better. Just the thought of lapping water sends calming waves through even my hardened, alligator skin.

As I return back to the master bedroom, and throw myself down on the silk sheets, I watch a salamander, if that's what it is, scurry out from behind a landscape picture, take one look at me, and then dash back under.

Clever salamander.

I guess the new level of creepy-crawlies is one thing that I hadn't accounted for coming out here to Brian's mansion in Spain, but one that I'm going to have to cope with.

That's right, Anna Harris: bloodthirsty, unfeeling assassin, is afraid of things that crawl about in the night.

Or in the daytime, come to think of it.

Later, when I take in the en suite, I'm certain that Brian has towel rails made out of ivory there. I wonder at them a few moments, and then turn back to give myself a good look in the sand-washed mirror.

Droopy eyelids?

Check.

Puffed-up lips and cheeks?

Check.

More wrinkles than three months ago?

Check.

If I can say nothing else about working for Brian, it's that he keeps me on my feet. Doesn't let me get a moment's rest.

Though this is going to be a real change of pace.

Just me, and a mansion, and the sea, all of us sinking into one another in a relaxing purple haze that the strongest of epidurals would be jealous of.

CHAPTER TWO

If there's another thing Brian can be counted on for, it's his love and —therefore—abundance of entertainment.

He has an entertainment system that, if Shakespeare had seen it, back when he'd been scratching about writing his plays, he might've simply thrown in the towel knowing that entertainment was destined to reach its pinnacle several centuries beyond his lifetime.

A *giant* plasma screen which stretches over the top of an open fireplace . . . though I'm scratching my brains as to why *anyone* would want to start a fire here.

Then again, I guess I'm yet to spend a night at the mansion, and maybe it whips up a chill at night.

There's surround sound, or whatever it's called when you seem to have speakers stuck up on every single wall, and sticking out from every single nook and cranny of a room.

Maybe that's what you'd call a cinema.

And an *enormous*, sleek white leather sofa sits in front of the screen. At least big enough to host a small street party . . . if there was anybody actually in the neighbourhood to invite over, since I didn't see any other houses on the narrow dirt track up from the main road to the mansion.

I can feel a yawn coming on and I tell myself to snap right the hell out of it. This is no time for napping. I'm not forty yet, because that's the first time that I'll truly allow myself to surrender to the temptation of napping.

And not a moment before.

They can go and strap on my giant nappy, and stick in my food drip at about the same time that I give in to napping.

A minimalist clock hangs up on the wall. Between speakers. All it consists of is two simple, black hands, and a series of black notches.

I guess that it's just a little after midday now.

I took an early-morning flight, and it took the best part of two hours to drive over to the mansion with Mr Talkative.

And if I've any hope of staying awake till teatime then I'm going to have to keep myself busy. Keep myself active.

So, with that thought on my mind, I decide to head down to the garage . . . one thing that Brian *did* tell me about, and something that I have no intention whatsoever of passing up.

Because, though I'm meant to be relaxing, I'm nothing if not a fidget.

And an explorer.

∗ ∗ ∗

Did I mention the heat?

I guess it might've slipped my mind somewhere in that indulgence of the whole damn mansion around me. And the whole thing of travelling from the airport in an air-conditioned car, and then stepping straight into the mansion.

But down here in the garage it's sticky.

Really sticky.

Stifling even.

Maybe before it wasn't kicking its way up thermometers, but it certainly feels that way now.

The garage smells vaguely of oil, and petrol. Maybe a little after-smell of leather there too. And that cinnamon that just seems to linger about the whole damn mansion.

Just *standing* here makes me feel thirsty, though I don't really think I am.

Down here I can still hear the aforementioned insects. Chirruping away in Spanish.

I wipe the sweat off my forehead with the long sleeve of my cotton V-necked top—beige, wasn't that adventurous?—and let loose a few puffs of air as I look over the choices spread out before me.

Car.

One of those four-wheel-drive monstrosities. Green-tinted windows. Like my escort's glasses this morning. A square shape with solid, almost proud, buttocks.

Also pretty much like my escort.

White. Just like the rest of the mansion.

The other transportation option is a motorbike.

White also.

It looks sporty.

And shiny.

But that's just about all it says to me.

I never knew that Brian rode at all . . . or maybe it's one of his mistresses that's keen.

Knowing him, he probably doesn't even remember that he's even *got* a motorbike here. But that's enough probing of Brian.

He *has* given me free roam of his mansion after all.

I think things over. Stare at the car and motorbike waiting in the shadow of the garage. And then I see the flourish of sunlight peeking in through the base of the folding-back garage door, and I know that going out in *that* in a pair of jeans would be a massive mistake.

Already I can feel the sweat oozing out of me. And impressing itself into the material.

Yup, think it's time to make a wardrobe change.

* * *

I decide to go with a white sundress. I guess there's some subconscious inkling hanging onto me trying to get me to blend in like a chameleon with the mansion.

It feels much better to wear the dress.

And it lightens my mood too.

I go with a simple pair of hazelnut-brown leather sandals too.

Flat-bottomed shoes are always a good choice when driving an unfamiliar car.

I crunch my way along the dirt roads at the wheel of the Four-by-Four Box Wagon, which I'm guessing isn't close to its *real* name. I never was very good with cars.

Caring about cars.

What I do know, though, is that the air conditioning is right up my street. It blows cool and fresh, carrying away any residue sweat still clinging to my skin.

And it dries my mouth out a little too.

Makes me thirsty.

But I tell myself that, soon, I'll be at the beach. And I can take care of that need.

I grip the leather steering wheel tighter as I come up to a few dastardly bends, and do my best not to glance over the steep drop over on my right-hand side.

Pretty soon, and probably against all odds, I make it to the battered-up asphalt road, with its yellow markings and the sand drifting its way across it.

I screw up my eyes at the blue signpost with its indications all in Spanish, and another language that I don't recognise.

Remembering my school Spanish lessons . . . or did I study French? . . . I take a right and head off on my way, having my suspicions confirmed by that glowing blue of the sea on the horizon.

I guess that means I'm on the right track.

* * *

There's a lot of empty brush land before I start to see the houses of the town. And see the sparkle of the afternoon sun on the deep, blue sea.

The houses are all painted in bright colours, although they're all a little faded from the sea breezes: all turquoises and hearty pinks, and cheese yellows.

All of their windows and doors blocked up with chipboard. I guess this is what happens in the off season. This place becomes bereft of life.

I notice the asphalt giving way to cobblestones pretty soon after, and I grip the steering wheel all the tighter.

If there's one thing that *always* unnerves a driver driving for the first time in a long while, it's when the road surface shifts around beneath you.

Well it unnerves me at least.

As I trundle the car down along the cobblestones, feeling every last bump of them both through the steering wheel and through my seat, I see the sign with a large and distinct 'P' for 'Parking.'

Now that's a language I can understand.

I follow it round, and *voila*, I find myself in an empty car park.

I suppose that's something of a mercy given that my parking skills have never been up to much . . . and, in this big brute of a car, I'm sure that they'd have been given a solid failing grade.

CHAPTER THREE

The car key fob's made for idiots. A tiny little picture popping up out of the plastic with a lock unclasped, and a lock clasped. I go with the clasped lock, and the car gives a little celebratory *toot* of its horn and flashes its amber lights a couple of times.

I like to think of that as a cheeky wink.

As I slap my way, in my sandals, across the battered cement surface of the car park, I can already feel the gentle caress of the sea breeze against my cheeks.

Blowing my white sundress against my body.

I have to admit that this is just about as close to heavenly as I thought I could get.

I can hear the lap of the tide too. Stroking the shore. Sucking back. And then *swooshing* in again, sending the blue-grey pebbles skittering over one another.

No one's swimming in the sea, and I didn't bring my swimming costume. And I've got no intention of stamping my arrival on this poor unsuspecting town by disrobing and going in wearing just my underwear.

Though it *is* just a little tempting.

Instead, I trudge my way along the promenade, or whatever it's called out here in Spain, and make for a tidy little hut, made out of dried rushes.

Its name is up there in peeling white paint on a weathered chunk of wood. *Por La Playa.*

A black waiter with a shaved head and a loopy, handlebar moustache stands wiping down a glass in his hands with a stained white cloth.

He gives me a curt smile, and then lays the glass down.

I take up a seat on one of the dark wooden stools that sticks up out of the ground on the end of a steel pole. Apparently cemented down so no one steals it.

"English?" he says.

I feel a slight quiver through my guts. "Is it that easy to tell?"

He gives a Gallic shrug—mouth pouting, shoulders rising in perfect time. "Jus' guess." He glances out beyond me, to the sea still lapping up on the shore. "You wan' something?"

I study his tone just a little. It sounds odd. Almost hanging. Maybe it's just his accent. The fact that English isn't his first language. That's most likely it.

Why would he have any reason to be mysterious?

. . . I guess I'm more shell-shocked than I thought. My mind still running on override. Threatening to pound all the adrenalin out of my body.

"Just something cool and fresh," I say, slightly enigmatically.

He bows his head and then turns round. He busies himself with the rows of upturned tumblers behind him, the sun reflected in their clear glass.

I can feel the sea breeze at my back, still blowing the dress against my skin. Like it's giving me some kind of gentle massage.

When he goes to squirt in what looks like rum, I ask him not to. He does that Gallic-shrug thing again, and then leaves the rum out.

Just filling the glass up with fizzy, bottled water. Then he lays the glass down on the hardwood counter and disappears off into the back of the hut, behind a manky, half-shredded curtain.

Not having any pretence to be polite is pretty nice, all told, so I take the opportunity to spin a one-eighty on the stool, and face off into the sea.

All alone here.

Just me and the lapping waves.

Who would've thought it just a week ago?

As I sip on my drink, which turns out to be fizzy water with a pinch of lime juice . . . I guess the intention of the rum was to give it a bit of a twist . . . I hear a car starting up. Back in the car park.

On instinct, because there's no one else about the sleepy village, I turn my attention towards it.

I see a car.

The car that brought me out to Brian's mansion this morning.

And the escort driving it.

All blond. Still wearing his sunglasses. And, above all, straight faced.

Maybe I'm still a little giddy from lack of sleep, or from that rush I always get from flying, I give him a prim, and *very* girly, wave.

He ignores me, takes a hard right, and slips out of sight, climbing the hill that leads up and out of the village.

With a shrug. A *Gallic* shrug, I decide later, I go back to staring out to sea.

* * *

Most likely the black guy who runs the bar thinks I'm something of a ditz. Because I sit there, up on that bar stool, for what must be about three or four hours, just watching the sea.

Watching it lap in and out.

Watching the sun blink off its waves.

But this is just what I needed. A time to simply shut down my brain. To leave everything behind.

To leave the . . . well, I suppose I could call it a *day* job, behind.

The sun's dipping on the horizon, and I'm slurping at the last of my lime and fizzy water, and lashings of ice, when I hear those obvious sounds of a man looking to shut down for the evening.

I guess that's one of the problems in coming out here in the off season: everything's shut.

I pay up, and he gives me a gentle nod, and the sliver of a smile, and I make off in the direction of the car.

That lime still hangs about on my tongue, and sends a *zing* through all my taste buds. As if it's shocking me awake. But it's not just the lime, though. I've always felt more awake at night. More active. My brain more switched on.

I always kill people at night.

Only when I get back in the car do I notice how fully the sea breeze has smothered me. Because the car smells all musky and synthetic. And everything from the seat to the steering wheel is warmed up.

It's funny, but I just sit there, driver's door open, for a long while, listening to the sea wash in and out. I don't want to start up the ignition. Get this brute's engine purring and cursing, blocking out that beautiful, *natural* sound of the sea.

But I'm going to have to.

Unless I want to walk, that is.

And so, with great regret, I power up the beast and I head off on my way, back along the cobblestones, up that steep incline, and out of the village.

On my way out I see the sign for the first time. The *name* of the place. And I commit it to memory.

San Floriano.

A nice place, all told.

* * *

Back at the mansion, I have a brief faceoff with the electric garage doors. I jab several times at a button on the key fob that I'm sure opens the doors.

But, after much swearing, I come to the conclusion that it doesn't.

Only when I drive on a little more, by way of experiment, do I realise that actually how the doors work is by motion sensor.

I guess Brian doesn't have too many worries about getting robbed out here.

Then again, I'm certain that, though it doesn't seem like it, Brian has absolutely top-notch security on the place.

I'm not quite sure whether that's unsettling or reassuring.

Maybe a bit of both.

As I swing the brute into the garage, taking care not to sideswipe the motorbike still propped up on its kickstand, I catch sight of the front doors to the mansion above me.

Wide open.

I think about that for a moment.

Wonder about it.

Did I leave them open when I went out?

Or has someone been inside?

I bring the car to a stop in the garage, switch off, then haul myself out, and up the interior stairs and up into the front hall of Brian's mansion.

Yep, the doors are definitely open.

The grapefruit setting sun peeping through the gap.

I turn my attention back to the hall, perhaps with half a mind to check for any signs of a break in . . . *footprints*, that sort of thing.

While I don't see footprints, I do see a package on the table.

A *white* package on the dainty little marble-topped table that seems to exist just for a vase of flowers.

Or a package like this.

The package is all done up with a silk white ribbon too, tied into a bow.

And my first thought is . . . *bomb.*

CHAPTER FOUR

My heart sticks in my mouth.

Beating and beating and beating.

It's all I can hear in my eardrums. So loud as to almost be like the *ticking* of a bomb.

That sour taste of limes has turned to a brutal, sharp feeling, like I'm chewing on razor blades. The evening wind which whips in through the wide-open oak front doors feels like it's stinging my cheeks. Snatching my breath away.

My body goes all cold, and then heats up.

Cold again.

The cinnamon scent of the mansion becomes stifling, overwhelming, and seems to be sending me spiralling down in a fit of nausea.

I clench my fists down my side, grit my teeth, and tell myself, *Anna, I think you're overreacting.*

I don't pay all that much attention to myself at first, but soon the message seems to get through to my legs. Seems to unfreeze them. And my ankles, feet, follow soon afterwards.

Before I really know what I'm doing, I'm approaching the white package, all wrapped up with its silk white bow, and about a million things are spinning through my mind.

And not one of them is intelligible.

But I keep going. As ever, natural selection in action.

Only when I'm standing right beside the package does any sense of survival instinct kick in. Every voice in my mind shouting at me not to touch it. To just turn around, and to bolt out of the mansion, to get away just as far as I can.

But that's not what my hands are doing.

My hands are reaching out.

Reaching out for the package.

* * *

My clear-varnished fingernails come into contact with it. Just a light *scrape* against its side. The package shifts just a little across the white marble surface.

But there's no explosion.

Maybe it's triggered by flipping the lid.

Only one way to find out.

My heart beats even harder in my throat. Almost drowns out my hearing now. But I still reach for the silk ribbon. Curl it in my grasp. And then, gently, and softly, undo the knot there.

The ribbon falls away.

Next, I reach for the sides of the lid. Strengthen my grip on it. And then, in a single, smooth action, prise it off.

No *boom*.

Not even a *tick*.

Guess this must be my lucky day.

Or maybe I'm just a little too tightly wound.

I examine the contents of the box. It doesn't take long. I mean, it's difficult not to notice the object wrapped up in white tissue paper inside.

At least it's difficult for someone like me not to notice.

A gun.

A handgun.

I don't even need to unwrap it.

I *won't* unwrap it.

I hesitate. Look back over to the wide-open front doors. Try to see some sort of a clue.

But there's nothing there at all.

Not even rising dust off in the distance. No trace of a car beating a retreat.

Then again, if someone had *recently* come to the mansion to deliver this handgun here, then I guess I would've run into them out there on the dirt track, as they made their way back to the main asphalt road.

A real mystery.

And one that I have no intention of solving.

If there's one thing my mother taught me when I was a little girl, it was not to open letters addressed to other people. And, I'm fairly certain, that this particular package is *not* addressed to me.

Or, at least, I don't want to receive it.

Got nothing to do with it.

I'm here to relax, not to work after all.

Right . . . *right?*

* * *

I leave the gun right where it is, on that white-marble-topped table out in the front hall. I'm not completely sure what my reasoning is, though, thinking about it, I guess that it's based on the concept of 'whoever left it there, will be coming back for it.'

Yeah right, what kind of world do I live in?

To try and get the gun off my mind, I head back upstairs to the master bedroom, paw through my suitcase for the second time that day . . . I've never been one of those girls that changes outfit every hour of the day, but I *am* on holiday after all . . . and I get hold of a swimming costume.

Not a bikini.

. . . Though I have to admit that I *did* pack one of those.

Even out here, in the middle of nowhere, I've got no intention of getting caught in my knickers. I guess that's just the way that I've always been.

Call me conservative, or whatever.

Call me a *killer* if you like.

There's no way of avoiding it. As I make my way back down the winding steps, I have to pass back through the front hall on the way to the swimming pool.

The gun is still there.

Back in its package. Lid on. Ribbon tied up in something resembling those knots I use to tie my shoes . . . whatever *those* are called.

I give another of my fledgling Gallic shrugs, and then trudge on through the mansion, outback to the swimming pool.

* * *

I guess in my preliminary investigations, I've found the perfect time to take a dip out here. I can confirm that the time between five and six is just perfect. Warm. Not too hot. And no sun to fry you up like a salchicha.

Back in the Army, I swam a lot in training. Did lots of it, in fact. I never did it competitively, never really felt the urge, though some of my commanding officers did have a go at making me try.

Swimming, for me, has always been about relaxation.

Just the slip of water over skin. The cool water slowing you down. And that overwhelmingly natural, odourless *smell* of water all around.

As the sun slinks down over the horizon for my first sunset of the holiday, I prop my arms up on the side of the pool, onto the sandstone. And I watch the sun go all the way down.

I breathe in the cool scent of the dusty breeze, and feel the ebbing warmth of the water lap up against my sides. And I listen to the *cher-rup-cherrup* of the insects all tuning up for their night-time concert.

This is just what I've needed.

Exactly what I've needed.

CHAPTER FIVE

Just as I predicted, those bugs keep me awake. Don't give me any chance at all of sleep.

And, in the course of the evening, after I've made myself some pasta with butter . . . not really feeling bothered enough to throw anything more complicated together . . . I lie back in my bed, silk sheets all scrunched up and kicked to the foot of my bed, and stare up at the ceiling feeling my brain wind around and around.

And there's only one thought there.

No prizes for guessing either.

The gun.

I'm thinking about the gun.

It'll still be down there, on the white marble table, in the front hall of the mansion.

At least I had the presence of mind to shut the front doors when I went to bed. Even though I'm fairly confident that Brian's security here is top notch, I've lived long enough in London to know that leaving doors wide open is just an invitation to trouble.

Or maybe I've just grown cynical in my old age.

If thirty-five is old age.

Probably was a couple of centuries ago.

The air, too, has got all stifling all of a sudden. And now sweat seems to ooze out of just about every pore on my body. I hope that Brian's got a good laundry service here, because I'm guessing that if I put my mind to washing silk sheets I'm only going to do a good job of ruining them.

That cinnamon scent is stronger too. Wafting over me. Making my nostrils tingle. In a way it's insulting my culinary skills. Like it's tormenting me about just what my cooking could be if I put my mind to it. If I could make myself *care* about it.

But I know that it's just me and my mind driving itself batty again.

The gun, though, my mind keeps spinning back to the gun. And I know that it'll still be there. That no one's going to swing by and take it away any time soon.

Or maybe, just maybe, if I slip away to sleep like a good little girl, and I go downstairs for my brekkie in the morning, the package won't be there.

It could be that I'm just overwrought, and my imagination's getting the better of me.

It *has* been a stressful few months.

And my brain *does* need a break.

So why can't I stop thinking about it?

Though there's no clock in the bedroom, I know that precisely thirty seconds have passed before I'm swinging myself out of the king-sized bed and padding my way along the marble landing.

At first I haven't actually admitted to myself just where I'm going, though there must be some part of me that knows only too well, and that's what drives me onwards, like some cartoon character that's being led to a kitchen by those smell lines drawn in the air.

I pad my way down those stairs, and up to the white package, still on its little table.

I hang back for a moment, as if already regretting having come this far. Having got myself out of my bed. But I know that there's nothing else I'm going to do.

I won't be able to sleep if I *don't* do it.

I reach out for the package, undo my primary-school knot and then I shuck the lid once more. Peer inside, even able to make out the form of the handgun in the night-time gloom of the mansion.

Before I can catch myself, I reach forwards, take hold of the tissue paper that surrounds the handgun, and then I lift it up.

Heavy.

Heavier than I thought.

And its grip is *rough*, even through the tissue paper.

I hold back for another moment. Think I hear a twitch out there, outside the mansion, somewhere off in the darkness that surrounds the house for miles around.

But no, it's nothing.

Just my imagination again.

As I unwrap the handgun from its tissue paper, I'm a little taken aback by the difference of the virginal white of the tissue paper, and the coal-black of the gun.

The gun almost blends into the night.

No shiny parts.

Holding the gun down at my side, only holding it with a limp-wristed grip, I peer into the package, and see that there's something else there. A magazine, stuffed full of bullets. All ready for the shooting. But that's not what catches my eye.

What catches my eye is the scrawled note. All done in curly handwriting. Written out in pink ink, as if—being a *girl*—that's the sort of thing I like.

I guess there's no doubt now just who this gun is intended for.

I snatch up the note, crumple it in my fist, and then stalk my way off into the kitchen.

Because I have no *idea* where the light switch for the front hall is.

* * *

With the sallow flicker of the kitchen lights above me, I smooth the letter down against the marble counter. And I read over the curly pink handwriting:

Dear Mrs Harris,

I think I might have a proposal that is attractive to you.

Please accept this gift as a token of my intent, and seriousness.

All the best,

RP

If there's one thing that gets my undies in a twist, it's when people add that extremely unnecessary, and slightly patronising, 'Mrs' to my name.

Okay, so I got married, once upon a time.

Had a couple of kids.

Still have the kids.

And acquired an ex-husband.

Never took his name, though. Not ever.

But, even through my annoyance, I know that that's not the thing I should be worrying my pretty head about right at the moment.

This *RP* character, whoever he is, should ring a bell with me.

But he doesn't.

Nothing at all.

I think a little harder, but it's pretty tricky to think straight considering that my brain keeps telling me to turn myself around, head back up those stairs, tuck myself into that beautifully crafted king-sized bed, with its silk sheets and all, and let myself drift off into some very pleasant—and well *deserved*—sleep.

Not yet, though.

I need to get this straight first, or I can be sure that I won't find any sleep till the sun's come back over the horizon, and those insects outside have finally shut their mouths . . . or their legs . . . or whatever it is they use to make that unholy racket.

RP. RP. RP.

I play with it a while.

RIP?

Rest In Peace?

Is it a threat?

. . . If it was a threat then it wouldn't stand much to reason this *RP* character giving me a gun. And some ammo. Or maybe he's a gentleman. Maybe he *believes* in a fair fight.

CHAPTER SIX

The creak of hinges brings me round.

Downstairs.

Those large oak front doors of Brian's.

Still feeling doped up from sleep, I shove the white silk sheets off my body. Who would've known that around the early hours of the morning the temperature in the bedroom plummets? I had to go scrabbling about in the pitch black, with only the slight streams of light from the moon to illuminate the gloom.

I come round slowly. Try to realise just what the *creak* of those hinges mean.

Someone at the front doors.

Someone *opening* the front doors.

That wakes me up quickly. I sit up straight, give a slight yawn and then paw about inside of my clothes and stuff I've junked on the floor, looking for my mobile.

Finally I get hold of it. Flip it on. Watch the start-up screen.

I haven't dared switch my mobile on since I landed in Spain. Memories of a holiday in France, when I was younger, struck me.

When I was away with Arnold and the kids. And we went to the beach every day even though the weather was foul. Slanted rain blowing in from all directions. Howling winds.

I think it might even have snowed . . . or at least hailed.

But I can still recall those rich and thick hot chocolates we'd all share after getting back into a nearby café. And how that made everything about the day okay again.

Sent warmth shimmering right through me.

And smiles dancing across our lips.

. . . But what wasn't jovial and dewy-eyed was my phone bill when I got back home. I remember thinking to myself at the time about how great it was to be able to call everyone up. To check in with Brian, and friends.

After that holiday I don't think I've *ever* felt neutral about the word 'Roaming' ever again.

And I only glance at the screen of my mobile long enough to get the time imprinted in my head—just after ten o'clock in the morning—then I flip it off again. Chuck it back on top of my clothes all screwed up at the foot of my white-wood bedside table.

I reach into the drawer of the bedside table. It opens with the *rasp* of its wooden runners. And the cinnamon fairy seems to have been working overtime in this particular nook of Brian's mansion, because I get a great hearty waft of it right up my nostrils.

I prowl about for the gun inside.

My fingers linger over it.

Feel its cold metal against my skin.

Though I know that now's probably not the time, I examine the gun properly in the daylight.

A pistol.

Forty-five calibre.

Semi-automatic, single-action . . . though I deal with almost nothing else.

Custom. Like nothing else I've ever seen.

It has a name etched into its grip.

Solecito.

And a gleaming sunrise in the background of the chrome-dyed logo. So I guess the name has something to do with a sun . . . or not, I'm not even close to being a beginner at speaking Spanish, though maybe I should look to rectify that considering that I'm actually here now.

And here for as long as I like.

I do a little more scrabbling for the magazine. Slot it right in, and then cock back.

Ready for action.

* * *

Funny to think of it, but I feel a little unwieldy clutching the pistol, *Solecito*, down at my thigh as I prowl along the marble-floored landing.

It feels like it's been a while.

As I come closer to the staircase, with its chunky marble steps that start off narrow before fanning out as they trudge downwards into the front hall, I come to a stop, press my back up against the wall.

And I wait.

My heart beats hard. My hands go slippery with sweat. And I'm sure that I must absolutely stink, though all I can smell is that relentless cinnamon odour.

I still haven't had a shower since I got here . . . though I did take a dip in the pool the day before, that's almost as good, or so was the belief back when I was in school.

And my mouth tastes stale. I need to brush my teeth. Breathe some life back into my half-asleep body.

I listen hard. Stretch my hearing. And I feel the pulse of blood pumping all around my body. All my muscles are tight now. My finger is itching as it rests on the trigger. Just wanting to relieve all that tension.

And I know that firing off a round—or a *few* rounds—is the only thing that'll make me feel normal again. Like a smoker taking a drag on the first cigarette of the day.

Or, in my case, the first cigarette in *months*.

Footsteps. I can hear footsteps. A gentle *slap* of shoes against the marble floor. The sound echoes all around the front hall down below.

I dare a glance around the corner. Down into the front hall.

Can't see anyone there.

They're not in view.

And the oak front doors are now sealed shut, only a dribble of sunlight making its way in around the edges, and penetrating the easy gloom of the front hall.

The white package still stands on the marble table, the one that should be used for a vase of flowers. The lid's off the package, and its insides are exposed. And I scold myself for not having done a better job of concealing the packaging that I received this gun inside.

And now I really am worried about what might happen. That if whoever's there sees that I've taken the gun, and it's the same person who delivered the package, then they'll *know* that I have it. They'll know just what they're dealing with.

And that means that, most likely, they'll be packing a gun themselves.

All of a sudden the sweat slicking up my skin seems to reach saturation point. A draught blows over the marble floors and a shudder passes right over me. My finger quivers on the trigger of the pistol.

And a shot rings out.

CHAPTER SEVEN

only realise I'm swearing under my breath when the ringing clears my ears. When I actually notice that I've been off in a daze for a while now.

For too long.

Too long if I want to stay alive.

There's a slight smell of gun smoke in the air. That's cutting into the cool cinnamon odour, in any case, and I have the slight taste of blood in my mouth.

For one dizzy moment I get to thinking that I've shot myself right through the bottom of the jaw. But I soon snap out of that one. Realising that if that was the case then blood would be running all over me. And I'd be in horrible pain.

But I'm not in pain.

Other than my ears, now doing that dull ringing thing, I'm fine.

Or, at least, I *think* I'm fine.

My eyes wander upwards. Up to the roof. And I see the bullet hole I've punched in the ceiling. A gentle dusting of plaster cascades down through the air.

My heart beats wildly.

And then I remember what the hell I was actually doing stalking about Brian's mansion. I remember that *someone* is downstairs.

And they're most likely armed.

I turn my attention back to the mansion. Listen hard.

Nothing. I can't hear anything.

Not so much as a snatched breath.

But why would there be?

If whoever's down there is a professional then surely they know just what they're doing. They know when their target has just made a fatal mistake. Given away both their hiding place and just what kind of weapon they're carrying.

I wait a little more. Another second ticks by. And another.

The sweat dribbles down my cheeks. Forms rivulets beneath my chin. And runs down into my sleeping t-shirt: a ragged, manky affair with 'Splitting Lambs' splashed across the front in garish purple and yellow.

I've had the t-shirt since I was a teenager and I have some memory of 'Splitting Lambs' being a band that I liked way back when.

Though I couldn't tell you what music they played.

Nothing like that.

I hear a *shuffle* of footsteps down below. More movement. And then a voice calls up the stairs.

"Señor Matt-*hugh*-son?"

I hold still. Study the voice.

A lady's voice.

An older lady's voice.

And then everything clicks into place. And I allow myself to calm down. The tension in my arms to drop. And my grasp on the grip of the pistol to give some.

The cleaner.

This must be Brian's *cleaner*.

* * *

I'm already halfway down the front hall steps, getting myself down to the point where they fan out the widest, when I realise that I've still got the pistol held down at my thigh. I act on it, sticking it into the waistband of my pyjama bottoms, and hope that the elastic will keep it snug against my lower back.

Long enough for me to explain things, anyway.

I pad my way, barefooted, down onto the marble floor, and then I round the staircase and head in the direction of the kitchen.

Where I heard the voice.

That scent of cinnamon is more overwhelming than it has been at any other time now, and as I arrive in the kitchen, take in the gleaming sun pouring in through the enormous windows, I think I've just managed to track the source of it.

A bronze-skinned lady, about five-foot nothing, and with wispy, faint, blue-purple hair, squints at me from beneath thick lenses. She carries a brown canvas shopping bag in one fist, and a key ring in the other.

Her lips are slightly parted as she says something in Spanish that I have no chance of understanding. And so I do just what's required of the Brit abroad.

I just stand there and grin.

"Señor Matt-*hugh*-son?"

"No," I say, with a shake of my head. "He is not here. He stayed— *stayed*—in England."

The lady squints a little harder at me and I see that the canvas bag that she holds tight in her fist has butterflies stamped all over it. All different colours against the brown backing. And I can see that, nestled within the canvas bag, are several bottles of what I believe to be cleaning fluids. All different colours.

Her setup seems pretty serious.

Lips parted, the lady lays the canvas bag down and then, with a slight *jangle*, deposits the key ring down on the kitchen counter. It clinks dully against the marble surface.

She puffs up her lips and then blows out a load of hot air, shaking her head as she goes about it, and giving her eyebrows a slight wiggle.

She mutters something under her breath in Spanish a word of which *might* be 'England.'

I wonder what I'm supposed to do now, and so I say, "See you later," smile hard at her, and then head off on my way, back up the stairs, to take that long-promised shower.

* * *

For the remainder of the morning, me and the cleaning lady make a good job of avoiding one another. I have a slight crisis regarding just where I should stash the gun, somewhere the cleaning lady won't stumble across.

In the end, I settle on my luggage. She'll have no reason to go in there. And I cannot believe that Brian will permit a cleaner employed on his property that has any inclination whatsoever to go prying into personal items.

His background checks are really that thorough.

As I shower myself with the provided shower gel, lemon-scented and, I'm sure, *extremely* expensive, I think over the cleaning lady's reaction to me.

Try to bring some logic to bear on the matter.

Then, all at once, I reckon that I've got it.

Surely this cleaning lady is accustomed to stumbling across strange women staying here in the mansion. I know for a fact that Brian flies his many mistresses about the globe for holidays, or whatever, and it would make sense that the cleaning lady thinks that *I'm* just another in this string of unending wenches.

Though I'm not sure how I feel about that assumption, I have to make peace with the fact that, unless I manage to suddenly master Advanced Spanish in the space of five minutes . . . and standing here under this steaming hot water of the shower, that doesn't sound terribly likely . . . I don't think that I'm going to have a hope of clarifying the situation.

Once I'm through with all my thinking, and my showering, I just give it another one of those Gallic shrugs, and decide that, really, there's nothing to be done.

I'm getting pretty good at those shrugs now.

Maybe if I do make a good go at Spanish I can pass for a local one day.

All lemon-scented and parched, and at last clean, I get myself dressed up in a pair of floaty trousers—not white today, just light blue—and a loose-fitting peach blouse. Then I slip on my brown leather-strapped sandals.

I listen at the door of the master bedroom for any sound of the cleaning lady still knocking about, and I hear nothing.

That's good.

At least one thing is going to plan.

I venture off down into the kitchen and find it just as deserted, though the cleaning lady's big canvas bag full of all her cleaning fluids is still there. Sitting on the floor.

I resist the temptation to unscrew the caps and sniff away to find out which is the liquid that emits that distinctive cinnamon odour, and then move on to take a look at the fridge.

Since the fridge blends into the rest of the white-wooded kitchen, it takes me a solid five minutes to finally locate it and, when I do, it has about three times the capacity of my own fridge back home.

I peruse the contents, find some cheese there, and some butter too, and I use my nous to flop together a very basic sandwich. As I'm feeling in a somewhat exotic mood, I even throw some sliced-up tomatoes into it too for good measure.

Once I've finished, that's when I do my wondering of just how that cheese, and the tomatoes, and the bread, came to be in the mansion. And why they haven't gone off.

Then I notice the plastic bags stuffed into the cleaning lady's canvas bag and finally put two and two together, realise that this cleaning lady is also in charge of keeping the mansion fully stocked for any guests that happen by.

I think about taking a drive, going off out to San Floriano again, but reconsider, not wanting to make a spinster image of myself with the barman too soon, because, before I know it, I'll be off out to the *Por La Playa* bar every day.

No, better to lie low for today at least, and I am feeling a little dozy still.

I guess I've got a lot of recovering to do.

And so, with the heat sweltering outside, and the bugs all buzzing their heads off, I decide to settle myself down on the white leather sofa in the sitting room, and to flip on the plasma TV.

When I do switch it on it's probably comparable to ogling your eyeballs right up against a nuclear reactor core.

Or, at least, that's how it seems to me.

* * *

At some point, while I'm watching the English-language film channel, I doze off.

When I wake up, the bugs are all going into overdrive, the air is thick—thick with *cinnamon*—and it's dark out. I blink away my extended siesta, and breathe in the stuffy air.

I glance up to Brian's minimalist timepiece, up there on the wall. In the sickly glow of the plasma TV I manage to cobble together a rough idea of the time—just after six o'clock is my best guess—and I force myself up off the leather sofa, and back up onto my feet.

Since I've been wearing my sandals all day, several red welts have appeared about the brown leather straps. I bend down and undo the clasps, reminding myself that, mostly, putting them on at all was some sort of a courtesy to the cleaning lady.

But now she's gone. Unless she's working a nightshift.

At the very least, when I return to the kitchen there's no sign of her canvas bag.

One thing there *is* a sign of, however, is a plastic-wrapped saucepan of what I recognise to be paella. Guess I'm not as mono-cultural as I thought. And I find myself almost instantly revising my opinion of the cleaning lady.

Because if there's one thing that can be said for people who not only cook, but have a habit of leaving leftovers . . . well, there's only one thing that can be said for such people.

'Angels,' pure and simple.

The plate's still warm and I guess that I haven't missed the cleaning lady by all that much. Once I've taken the paella down, I feel far more awake.

And though I'm sure my breath absolutely stinks of garlic now, and of fish . . . not usually a fetching combination, I find that I really don't care at all.

I'm out here, all alone, and I've got this whole damn mansion to myself.

Only when I'm headed up the stairs, and looking forwards to my impending night swim . . . I'm wondering if tonight's the night I finally give up on the swimming costume, and allow myself to enjoy the fact that there are no neighbours overlooking the house . . . do I remember the whole business of the white package. And the gun.

I turn back, halfway up the stairs, glance down at that small marble-topped table in the front hall. No sign of the package. Just a nice, pleasant-smelling vase of flowers, and I've no idea what they are . . . though they're yellow if that helps.

I guess the cleaning lady did a thorough job after all.

That makes me pause, though. And a prickling feeling extends all over the surface of my skin. I feel on edge now. Totally the opposite of how I was meant to feel here in Brian's mansion. And I wonder whether, if I really have the intention of relaxing properly, I should jam myself back into the Box Wagon and head off to some hotel.

It's not like I couldn't afford it.

And it *would* give me peace of mind.

Though leaving this mansion *does* seem like a real waste.

But maybe my peace of mind is more important.

Of course it's more important.

So, with that resolution occupying my mind, I decide that tomorrow I'll head off somewhere else.

Somewhere I can be sure that Brian won't be watching.

CHAPTER EIGHT

Nothing about the morning feels good.

My head is spinning worse than any morning sickness I've ever experienced in my life. And my guts feel like they want to turn themselves inside out for good.

I just about make it to the toilet without slamming myself unconscious against one of the white-washed walls of the master bedroom.

There's no way of knowing just how long it takes before I feel like I've got my feet firmly back down on the ground and, even then, when I feel like I have returned to Earth, my mind is still protesting against the confines of my skull.

The bitter taste of vomit lies beneath my tongue. And that stench of cinnamon is ripe and prickles the insides of my lungs.

Already I can feel the air about me heating up, and it only serves to send my nausea spiralling down further, deeper, into the very base of my guts.

As I stumble on my way across the marble floors, vaguely headed for the kitchen, the only sounds that I can make out around me are the slapping of my feet and the cacophony of my breathing as it catches my blocked nose.

Guess I brought some kind of lurgy along with me from home.

And then I think back to the paella, from the day before, and I suppose that *that's* most likely the cause of all this.

As I scour the cupboards for a glass so that I can at least wash away the vomity taste from my mouth, I get to wondering whether the cleaning lady poisoned me on purpose.

Would she do something like that?

. . . I don't know her.

Maybe, if she really believes that I'm another of Brian's endless stream of women, she has built up a strong resentment for the visitors here, and that makes me wonder why.

Is it because they're . . . *we're* . . . rude to her? Or is it because we don't speak her language, don't even *try?* Or maybe it's really nothing at all to do with *us* and more to do with what we represent. Maybe she just sees us as some sort of invaders, arrived here to do away with everything she loves about her hometown.

I wish I knew enough Spanish to reassure her of that.

Once I get my hands on a glass, I try to catch myself, to make myself see just what sort of paranoid thinking I've got blazing through my skull.

Am I really serious?

I mean, *really?*

A kindly old lady, most likely somebody's granny, who comes out here to Brian's mansion to clean and to bring in supplies, groceries, would really be interested in making whoever's staying here suffer?

. . . I guess I have grown cynical in my old age . . . no, wait, scratch that . . . that should just be plain misanthropic.

* * *

And so goes my third day at Brian's Spanish mansion. Me, the world spinning a little faster than I'm comfortable with, dashing for the toilet at the slightest twitch of the stomach, and the bugs outside croaking their heads off.

Sometimes life just kicks you when you're down.

And then kicks you again.

It must be the early evening by the time I get my head back together in some sort of a logical state, and I take myself up for another shower, to get shot of any lingering feelings of the food poisoning . . . or maybe it *was* just from some bug I brought along with me from Blighty . . . and I get myself done up all pretty and sweet, and in a cool little black number.

One that I've reserved for truly special occasions.

A dress that'll blow all the cobwebs away and get me back onto firm ground, which is just what I need right at the moment.

I dig out a pair of matching black plimsolls, too, and I jab my feet into them. Walking around barefoot has always been a bad habit of mine. Something that I've done on instinct. And it does mean that it takes a little longer in the shower than it should, to get shot of all those shabby little shreds of lint and all those pieces of grit.

Tonight, I've decided, I'm going down to San Floriano, back down to the beach. To see the sea in the moonlight. It's the least I deserve after the day I've had.

And so I load myself up in the Box Wagon, pile on out of the drive, and do my best not to roll the car into one of those steep slopes that lie to the right-hand side of the dirt driveway which leads out to the main road.

* * *

Feeling refreshed, the sea breeze having blown back my hair, and also seeming to have blown away any of those lingering sensations of nausea, I watch the twin yellow gleams of the headlights dance across the front of Brian's mansion.

Back home.

I wait for the electronic *groan* of the garage doors and then deposit the Box Wagon in its rightful spot, beside the motorbike, before climbing the stairs and arriving back in the front hall.

As I pass over the cusp of the marble step, already feeling the cool draught blowing through the corridors of the mansion, I half-expect to see the vase of flowers missing from that marble-topped table, and another white package lying on top of it.

Complete with the silk ribbon like before.

There's nothing there, of course.

Only my overactive imagination just trying to keep me occupied.

I wander my way through the house, back to the kitchen again. I don't want to flick on the lights, the moonlight is just so beautiful, almost like a film set. I don't want to break the illusion.

In the kitchen, I pour myself a glass of water, tepid obviously from having sat in a sun-baked pipe all day, but it tastes just fine as I glug it down.

That's one thing about being here. You get so used to sweating that it can be hard to remember that you've got to keep taking on fluids. And that sounds just like something I'd chide my kids for not doing . . . and maybe that just goes to prove what a crappy parent I am.

Everything's quiet. Even the bugs tonight. Not so much croaking.

The air's lighter, and the cinnamon smell is less pronounced, though it's still there, like a *really* bad neighbour constantly peering over the back garden picket fence.

I give the water a good slosh about my mouth, getting it into all my gums, making sure that they're all appropriately hydrated, and then I turn to head out of the kitchen.

The idea of going for a swim lingers on my mind. Just for a moment. And then I think better of it.

Not ready for bed yet, though, I decide to go and numb my brain a while with Brian's nuclear TV, and I step my way through the darkened house, lit only with moonlight, into the sitting room.

And, right there, standing in the shadow, off in a corner of the room, is the escort.

The escort who brought me here.

CHAPTER NINE

The first thought that skitters through my mind is the gun. That it's upstairs. Hidden away in my luggage. And then I wonder to myself just what good it can do there.

None at all, that's what.

Though I can just about make out his face in the moonlight which drifts into the sitting room, I can't see his hands at all. They're cast in shadow.

I wonder if I can make a swift turn. If I can somehow manage to backtrack the four or five steps. Head back into the front hall. Then up the steps. Sprinting all the way to my room.

But I've got a feeling if I try that I'll be dead before I hit the floor.

And so I turn my mind to democracy. I stare through the gloom, doing my best to meet his eyes, and I say, "You've come to take me to him, haven't you?"

The escort makes no reply. I wonder if he understands. If he doesn't then there's really nothing at all I can do. It's not like I can clear this all up with a flourish of Spanish.

The house sits in silence, as if in reverence to our meeting, realising that pretty soon there might be blood spilled over its white marble floors.

And that would be a nightmare for the cleaning lady to get out.

The smell of cinnamon overwhelms everything as if having had the house sit in the sun all day has brought whatever substance, or cleaning fluid, causes it right to the surface of everything. My lips are a little dried up from the salty sea breeze, and my toes are covered in sand from where I waddled into the waves.

The escort just stands there, in the darkness. Now he's really starting to creep me out, and yet I have no idea what to do next. What he *expects* me to do. Maybe this is the plan. That he wants me to make the first move. Whoever this *RP* character is, perhaps they're just waiting for some reason to kill me . . . some reason he can explain to Brian because, surely, given that Brian had this escort come here to meet me at the airport, they must have some sort of relationship.

Now I find myself cursing getting ill this morning, having eaten that paella the day before. I could've been away by now. A *long* way away.

Somewhere Brian would have no chance of getting to me.

But, instead, I'm here, standing in the sitting room, and facing off with this escort.

All of a sudden, and without a word, the escort shifts out of the shadows, steps his way carefully across the marble floor. As he does so, my heart raps harder, and I get a chance to see him better in the moonlight.

No gun.

That's the first relief.

But no smile either.

He seems to be wearing the same black suit as he did at the airport, when he drove me here to the mansion. This time, though, he doesn't wear a tie. His cream shirt is open two buttons at the neck. That makes sense given the heat. I've always thought that people who wear ties in hot places are just a few eggs short of a dozen.

He draws closer to me. I catch a whiff of his cologne. And he holds his shoulders in a huddle, the suit hardly up to the job of keeping all his muscles inside. He meets my eye briefly and I see they're grey eyes . . . or at least they seem that way in the moonlight.

Then again, I suppose *everything* looks grey in the moonlight.

For a brief second I'm sure that he's going to reach out and grab me, snatch hold of my forearm, and yank me off after him. And I know there'll be nothing I can do.

I never was all that great when it comes to self-defence.

Not without a pistol in my hand, anyway.

But he doesn't take a hold of me, he simply brushes past, less than a pace between us, and he makes his way off into the front hall. Makes for the front doors of the mansion.

I wait with my heart lodged in my throat, watching him head away from me.

A voice inside my head is screaming. Telling me that *now* is my chance.

Now I can rush upstairs, go grab *Solecito*. Then things will be a little more even. I'll actually have a cat's chance in hell of getting out of this place alive.

When he reaches the heavy oak doors, he slides the latch upwards. The *scrape* of metal on metal shudders through the front hall. Over the marble floors. And it sends a skitter down my spine. And makes my gut dip.

Then he tilts his head back to me in a way that can be nothing else other than an invitation to follow.

He wants me to go with him.

Of course he does.

And if I don't follow then, I'm sure, he'll have orders to kill me.

Lucky for me, though, my bravery shines through once again, and I manage to raise my voice to the escort once again. "Can I .

. . uh, can I go get something." I point upwards, as if that's going to help with understanding here. "From upstairs?"

He harnesses me for a long moment with those doleful, grey eyes of his and then he gives me a slight nod. So slight as to be nigh on imperceptible.

But I perceive it.

Because I've seen my chance. My chance to at least have *something* to fight back with.

* * *

From upstairs I grab a handbag, black leather with silver buckles, to match my dress, though I'm sure that's not where my conscious thought is focussed.

And I dig about for the gun—for *Solecito*—and turn it up in my luggage, before stuffing it into my handbag.

I hesitate a moment, wondering whether I should throw something else into my handbag, make some kind of an effort to conceal the gun. But what would be the point?

RP, this guy, this *escort*, working for RP, surely he knows just what I'm packing anyway. Most likely he was the one to bring the gun here in the first place.

I did see him on the beach at San Floriano that first day here. And he left soon after he saw me arrive there.

Had he just been waiting for me to clear out of the mansion so he could slip by surreptitiously?

Maybe.

But that hardly matters now.

I follow the escort out of the front doors and around the house to where I find he's parked up his car—the same one that brought me from the airport, of course.

Maybe it's because I don't care all that much about cars, or maybe it was because when he picked me up I was half-asleep, but I hadn't fully taken into account just how *big* the car actually is.

It's a turtle-shell green, with tinted windows, of course, and there is a sliding door which leads to the passenger seats in the back. A *van* really.

I guess I didn't notice those seats on the way from the airport because I was sitting up front. I've always found it weird to have someone drive you and to sit in the backseat . . . leaving the front passenger seat empty . . . kind of like having a chauffeur or something.

He zaps the car. It blinks its lights and toots its horn in a way that reminds me of the Box Wagon. And I can't help feeling, as I take the big step up to the front passenger seat, the escort holding the door open for me, how much I miss that big, old brute.

At least with the Box Wagon *I* was in the driver's seat.

* * *

The car . . . *van*, smells just as much of that distinctive new-car smell as it did on the way from the airport. I wonder how often the escort has the car shot off to be valeted. Maybe he has some sort of a cleanliness complex. OCD?

I gaze at the escort in profile, see his stubbly chin, those grey eyes glinting in the moonlight. He has that classically chiselled jawline, and that tuft of blond hair seems to be just about the only softness about him.

Even despite the overpowering new-car smell, I still find that I can't get shot of that *damn* cinnamon taste in my mouth. I wonder, when I finally do go home from this open-ended holiday, whether when I'm unpacking my suitcase that cinnamon stench will waft up at me, find its way into my house.

We bomb along the dirt path, way too fast for my liking, and towards the main road. I feel every bump in the road. That's the annoying thing about being a passenger, that you feel *everything*.

The tyres grip and crunch their way along, and I listen to the *ping* of rocks bouncing off the bottom of the car, and I reconsider my first appraisal of the escort being some kind of OCD case. Because, surely if he was, he would be paying a lot more attention to those dents surely being banged into the paintwork.

The steep drop on the right-hand side doesn't get any better whatsoever being sat on the passenger side of the car, and I feel my stomach drop away, and try to make myself busy staring off from beneath the windscreen to the unwinding road ahead.

We don't head for the coast, taking a left turn instead of the right towards the sea, and the escort picks up speed, goes even faster, as the tyres touch the sturdier asphalt surface.

I can't resist glancing back over my shoulder, looking back to the dirt path, and to the mansion, standing proud like a white-washed mausoleum in the otherwise impenetrable darkness.

And I wonder if this is going to be the last time I'll see it.

* * *

We drive on for a long while. Maybe an hour. Maybe a little more.

For the first ten minutes or so I make a point of scoping out landmarks, stones lying at the side of the road, strangely formed trees, and then drop it soon after when I realise that we've just been headed along the same road—the road that leads to the sea—the whole while.

If the worst comes to the worst. If I have to *walk* back to the mansion, I'll be able to guide my way by following this well-built road.

I look to the fob on the door, see that it's unlocked. There's nothing keeping me here, in this van. But, then again, if I toss myself out here I'll be in the middle of nowhere. And the only places I really know around here are Brian's mansion and San Floriano.

And I would've thought RP would easily be able to pick me up from either spot.

Bring me back in.

Then again, maybe RP is reasonable.

Perhaps he'll listen to me.

The escort declutches and slows the car down far too fast for my stomach's comfort. It feels like I've left it a mile or so behind. Then he takes a hard left off the road, heading along another dirt path—pretty much identical to the one which leads to Brian's mansion—and we begin that horrible swirling motion upwards over rocky terrain.

I feel that nausea from the morning making a re-entrance, and I crunch my teeth together, seal my eyes tight, as if that'll make it go away. It does help, just a little bit. But I can still taste that warm bile brimming its way up my throat.

I'm extremely glad when the escort finally brings the car to an abrupt halt, the tyres sliding over the loose dirt, sending yet more pebbles up and pinging off the paintwork.

That's when I open my eyes.

Open my eyes to see our destination.

Nothing.

Just dirt.

CHAPTER TEN

All other thoughts desert my mind. I don't care about being subtle any longer. About not showing my hand. Because they *know* my hand. The escort *knows* my hand.

And I know just what this looks like. This sight spread out before the bonnet of the van.

Dirt. In the middle of nowhere. Only moonlight.

Can it be anywhere else but a burial site?

I shoot the escort a sidelong glance. Try to read his expression in profile in the moonlight. But he gives nothing away. Nothing at all. He just stares out in front of him, hands still clasping the steering wheel. The only motion that disturbs his face is the occasional blink.

I look down to my handbag, in my lap. And I scrabble for the zip. Bring it back with a gentle rippling sound.

I look to the escort. No reaction. Still facing forwards.

This is my chance.

Now or never.

Blood rushes to my head, and I can taste it in my mouth. Throbbing through my tongue. The new-car smell has a strangle hold on me. The engine continues to run. Ticking along. And I can feel a prickling shudder as the cool air from the ventilation ducts brushes over my skin. Sends all my hairs erect.

I paw through my handbag, fingers clasping about the pistol grip.

And then, in a smooth motion, I slip it out, raise it straight in my arm, and hold it to the escort's temple. "Don't you move," I say.

No reaction from the escort. Hands still on the steering wheel. Staring straight forwards.

Thinking about it now, it seems almost like he's prepared for this. As if he's assuming the position. Thought this through. Thought that I'd want to see his hands. See that he wasn't going to make a quick move for the inside of his jacket. Pull his own gun.

My heart pounds harder. My blood runs slicker. And hotter. "Understand?" I say. "Do. You. Understand. Me?"

Again, no reaction from the escort. Just that infuriating stare forwards. That neutral expression pressed on his lips.

I decide that it's time to experiment. "Hands on your head," I say.

Gradually, he does what I ask. Perfect. No chance for his motion to be misinterpreted. He peels each finger off the steering wheel, out of those ruts impressed in the leather, and he gently lays his hands down over his blond hair.

Still staring forwards.

Most likely it's the adrenalin, but I find myself smiling. A *wry* smile. "All right," I say, "now that we're getting some way to understanding one another, how about you turn and look at me straight on? Or is there something devastatingly interesting about that dirt out there?"

The escort remains facing forwards.

Maybe he has selective hearing.

I have a remedy for this desease.

I give the pistol a little shunt. Just a little press into his temple. Like giving a horse a squeeze with your heels. Just reminding it that you're still there. Riding on top. In control.

Slowly, the escort turns his head. At first his grey eyes keep up their steady, directionless gaze, but soon enough they snap onto mine. And I see the moon reflected in their glassy surface. "So," I say, "what's supposed to happen now?"

No reply, surprise, surprise.

I give him another nudge with the gun. "There a light in here?" I say.

He stares back at me, his expression still totally neutral. He blinks a long blink and then, right hand leaving his head, reaches up to the roof. To a whole array of switches. He snaps one of them back. A blinding, yellowish light floods the inside of the car.

Purple dots appear on my vision, but I concentrate on keeping the gun pressed up against the escort's temple. Watch him replace his hand back down on his head. Make *sure* that he hasn't tried anything. Tried to sneak something or other out of the sunshade.

If I wanted to keep a gun handy, that's where I'd put it.

One of them anyway.

I'm on the point of asking him again, of jostling him for answers once more, when I hear the distinctive *crunch* of gravel. The grind of another engine. Another car making its way up the dirt path.

In that moment I just forget everything, forget I've got a pistol pressed to a guy's forehead—for God's sake!—and I glance back over my shoulder.

A car, much smaller, no more than a common city hatchback, climbs the slope, its headlights a pair of cat's eyes.

It shuffles its way upwards, slowly but surely, not possessing any of the power that this van has. Finally, it slows and slides up alongside us.

The driver switches off the engine.

All that remains is the *growl* of the van's engine. The blow of the ventilators. And the *thrum* of my heart in my ears.

Only then do I look back to the escort, see that he's looking right where I'm looking, watching for the lady who's stepping out from the hatchback.

A young lady. Maybe about my age. Or perhaps a little younger.

I never did learn to age gracefully.

* * *

As the young lady draws closer to the car, I see that she has fair skin, and black hair with blond streaks. She wears a cropped brown leather jacket, which exposes the square-shaped belt buckle which holds up her denim cut-offs.

She's definitely younger than I first thought.

Seventeen?

Eighteen?

Early twenties?

Much younger than me, anyway.

She wears cosmic-blue tights that glint a little in the moonlight. She tops everything off with a pair of ankle-high boots that look like they've been borrowed from her brother. They are mud-spattered and the laces are undone and half torn-up, and they jiggle as she walks.

Only when she's about half a dozen paces from the side of the van, from my window, do I remember that I've still got the pistol pressed up against the escort's head, and that the interior light is switched on, broadcasting our pose to the outside, for anyone who cares to see. Which means this little lady.

She arrives at my window with a neat smirk, and she makes a loop-the-loop motion with her index finger. I take that to mean that I'm meant to wind down the window, though I don't believe a van like this has a winder . . . it'll be a button somewhere.

I decide to take a leap of faith and let the escort alone for now. As long as I've got *Solecito* snug in my fist I don't think there's all that much harm that can come to me. If this young lady has a whole troupe of heavies stuffed into the backseat of that hatchback then it's most likely curtains for me in all events.

Most likely.

The escort makes no reaction to me removing the pistol from his temple, though I don't know why I'd expect him to make so much as a move. He's been so slick cool throughout the whole palaver.

Holding the pistol in my favoured right hand, I reach out for a button that looks likely to bring down the windows.

Eureka.

With a mechanical *whine* the window winds down and the cool night breeze floods in. The air out here, in the middle of nowhere, smells pretty similar to the air at Brian's mansion. Which is to say, it smells of dirt.

For some inexplicable reason my mind flashes back to a time at school, maybe it was a PE lesson, something like that, but the upshot of the recollection was me, face down, in some stirred up, baked dirt.

I think I can still taste it in my mouth. Some of it still engrained into the insides of my cheeks.

The young lady reaches out to me and rests a supple, spindly wrist down on my window ledge. And she meets me with her rosy brown eyes. "You mus' be Anna Harris," she says, her words thick with her Spanish accent.

"What gave me away?"

The girl smirks a little wider. Gives a little Gallic shrug of her own. Maybe I could learn a thing or two from her because, the way she does it, the way she cocks her head slightly to one side, and makes a few dimples appear in her chin, is the stuff of mastery.

"I believe," she says, "it was you wit' the gun against Germo's head."

The way she pronounces 'Germo' is with the 'G' like an 'H' sound. And I can vaguely recall something about Spanish pronunciation related with that.

But it skitters back out of my mind just as quickly.

Germo, it follows, is the escort.

"Yes," she says, "I believe tha' was it."

I shoot Germo a glance over my shoulder, and only when I turn back to the young lady do I wonder if there was a slight note apology there.

Not impossible.

"And you're RP?" I say.

"No," she says, her eyes still deeply buried within mine. "No, I am no'."

I look past her. To the hatchback. Now I realise that I can see inside. That, unlike what seems like just about every other vehicle around here, it doesn't have tinted windows. I can see into the backseat.

No huddled-together cronies.

I allow myself to relax an inch before mounting my pissed-off face, and pointing it directly at this girl. "Look," I say, "I'm tired, I've been ill today, and I just want to get some rest. Why don't you just tell me what this about and then we can all go home?"

"Yes," she says, with a slight pout. "Of course I understand. I know that it can be tiring to travel. I have done a lo' of travelling. I travelled a lo' with my father, you see. And I was in a lo' of international schools."

I guess that's why her English is so good.

"And I promise tha' it will not be long before you can go home, back to that *wonderful* mansion. Back to those silk sheets, and to the, uh, swimming pool."

I have to admit that the swimming pool does seem mighty inviting right about now. But I don't let that thought interfere with my pissed-off face.

The young lady peers into the car, gives me a once over, just like some sort of a lowlife bar rat might. When she comes up for air she's grinning ear to ear. "You have got *awfully* well dressed for tonight."

I resist the urge to deliver a left hook to that dainty, know-it-all chin of hers. But only just. "I like to make a good first impression," I say.

She glances over the roof of the van, and off into the distance. "Good, that's good."

I suppress the temptation to look back over my shoulder. To see just what she's looking at. If there's one thing I've learned well, it's that when I've got a gun in my hand, it's much better to keep your eye fixed on your opponent. Because you never know when they'll attempt to steal a march on you.

Even a sweet-seeming girl like this one.

"Anna," she says, "may I call you 'Annie?'"

"No, I hate it when people call me Annie."

She gives me a slightly bug-eyed stare, lips pursed in an O-shape, and for the first time in our meeting I feel bad about my sour tone. But only for a fraction of a second.

"*Anna,*" she says, "Germo has brought you here tonight because I wanted to make you an invitation."

"Really?" I say, tightening my grip on the pistol and, at the same time, feeling the weight of Germo's glare upon me, knowing that now, more than any other time in our acquaintance, he is paying sincere attention.

"Have you ever been to a bullfight?"

"No, and I wouldn't really be interested either."

"Yes," she says, with a sly grin, "tha' is what the foreign people often say. They do not like to see the animals harmed. But I think it will be a good experience for you. A good cultural experience for you. It must get *awfully* boring in tha' mansion. A long way away from everyone."

"Not really, I quite like being alone."

"Still," she says, her tone quickening, as if there's some place that she's got to be, "it would be a good opportunity for you to meet the rest of my family, and to, uh, to . . . learn about how we might get to know one another a little better."

"What makes you think I want to get to know you any better?"

"Because we have a business proposal for you."

I feel a chilly sensation pass through my blood. Centre into my heart. And it's like a sickness burrowing right down to my stomach. I wonder if I'm going to vomit again, but I hold back. I meet her steely, unwavering gaze with one of my own. "No," I say, but it only comes out as a raspy whisper. "I . . . I . . ." just as I'm on the point of saying that I don't do this sort of thing any more, I find my mind doing a U-turn, backing down, and I finish up saying, "I'm on holiday."

"Yes, of course," she says beaming. "Which is why my family would like to entertain you. We would be *privileged* if you would accept our invitation."

"Who is your family?"

For the first time, she dials down her smile, even takes on a slight frown. "Oh, you shall meet them."

I can feel both her and Germo's eyes weighing down on me. And I know that, even with a gun in my hand, this is one of these situations where nothing good is going to come of saying no. And I reason, at least by saying yes, it'll get them off my back for a while.

So I face up to her, and say, "Okay."

She claps her hands together and does a tiny jig, from one foot to the next, as if she's sixteen years old and just been invited to the most popular girl in school's birthday party. "Wonderful," she says. "Wonderful, Anna."

And with that, she's already backing away, headed back towards the hatchback, somehow not tripping over in those clunky boots. "We see you on Saturday," she says, ducking down into the driver's seat.

Just before she shuts the door, she adds, "Remember to bring a hat. And some sun cream. It is very hot there. In the bullring."

As I watch her hatchback start up. Trundle back along the dirt track and away from us, I find myself turning to Germo, meeting his grey eyes, and seeing something of a sparkle there.

Just about the closest thing to life I've read in him this whole time.

And I wonder just what I'm in for.

CHAPTER ELEVEN

The next day, with the sun streaming in through the wide-open balcony doors of the master bedroom, I set about folding towels, making the bed.

Something that I almost never do . . . no, scratch that, something that I *never* do.

Towels fulfil their basic functionality all screwed up and stuffed into drawers just fine, same with unmade beds, or at least that's what I've found.

The bugs croak away out there in their hiding places among the tall grasses, and I watch for the sea on the horizon, telling myself that I'll head down there later, spend some serious time at *Por La Playa* with a cool, non-alcoholic drink in my hand, slice of lemon, or lime, perched on the side of the perspiring glass.

Today the air's a little cooler, easier for me to bear, in any case, and all I have is nice, clean sweat sopping out of my pores, and keeping me from overheating. And I guess the strength of that synthetic cinnamon scent might be inversely proportional with the distance the cleaning lady is away from the mansion. Or maybe it's because I have every window in the house wide open to let it out, and the fresh air in.

Time just seems to dribble by. Neither here nor there. Stopped almost.

That's one of the funny things about being on holiday. That way you just totally lose track of the days. For some reason, back in that car, tottering up in the middle of nowhere with only dust stretching around for miles, I got the impression that the next day, or the day after that, would be Saturday.

Nope. When I met with the girl, whose name I didn't even catch, and I was too exhausted to think to try and bleed a word out of Germo, I thought that I would only have a little time to wait for the bullfight.

But that was only Monday. And I have a whole week still stretching out ahead of me.

Maybe she was serious about wanting me to be well rested, and genuine in her sympathy for me being here, on holiday.

All the same, I can't help but think just what might've happened if I'd said no to her. If I'd simply put my foot down.

Would she have asked for the pistol back? Wanted *Solecito* returned to her possession post-haste?

. . . Or to whoever's possession it came from.

It could've got ugly really fast up there. And I wouldn't have been putting money on any one of us. Even if I'd somehow managed to extricate myself, even having to take down the girl to do so, I have absolutely no idea just who I'm dealing with here.

The type of people I'm dealing with.

I have no idea where they have eyes and ears, or just exactly what they know about me.

And I'm quite aware that I'm simply doing my best to justify my actions, when I know that I was simply feeling too worn down, too tired out, to say no. To take on that fight.

To take on a fight now.

My mind spirals with just what this *Germo*, this girl and her family want with me.

Well, one thing I have down for pretty much certain.

They want me to *kill* for them.

They've heard the Great Anna Harris is in town, and they want to see just what all the fuss is about.

Guess someone should've told them that, lately, her Kill Switch has been on the blink. That she's lost that cold-hearted killer's instinct. The one that made her famous in the first place. The one that got her into this whole heap of trouble.

And, if there's any justice in the world, the one that'll get her out of it now.

* * *

I pack a beach bag, feeling about ten, fifteen years younger while I do it. I picked out the beach bag from the airport, something I never thought I'd do . . . buying luggage from an airport, I mean.

It's a neat canvas bag, kind of like the one the cleaning lady has, except that it's a brilliant white—a good thing considering the colour scheme of the mansion—and has a blue design of something or other crawling up the side of it.

I see that Brian doesn't seem to do fluffy, well-washed beach towels, and I have to settle for one of the countless quilted bath towels.

White of course.

Hopefully the cleaning lady has some powerful soapsuds to fix whatever damage I'm inevitably going to do this poor quilted bath towel. It can't ever have imagined, in its little bath towel life, that it might see the rugged terrain of a pebble beach.

Life's a bitch.

I get changed into my swimming costume then throw on a light blue blouse and a white skirt. I think I read somewhere about light colours doing wonders for seeing off bity bugs, though I don't think I'd be able to point to any scientific evidence.

I don't forget the sun cream either, sliding a bottle inside too, and smelling that odour that's always had a knack of twisting my guts, though I'm not sure why. That warped, creamy smell, almost like moisturiser, but with some sour twist to it. And don't get me started about having to spread it over your skin.

Might as well slick some butter all over yourself.

I get a little twitchy as I move through the mansion. It just seems awfully *big* now. Just for me here. And having witnessed Germo sneak into here without me so much as hearing, well that's just put me right on edge.

Enough on edge to *always* walk about the house packing *Solecito* somewhere about my person. Ready for the quick-draw if required. And I've had to remind myself, whenever I've heard a stirring of twigs, or the *crunch* of some frog biting it from some predatory bird, that the cleaner might just pop in any day, and it'd probably be better for the both of us if I don't accidently pop a bullet in her forehead.

It'd make a horrible mess for one.

And so, just like normal, I head off for San Floriano, in the Box Wagon, beach bag lying on the passenger seat.

For the first time since I've got to the mansion, I feel like I'm at home. Which is strange, considering that I've got some unknown, and potentially extremely deadly powers watching over me, and a lingering visit to a bull-slaughtering show all planned out.

But somehow that doesn't cut into my riding-high mood as I push the pedal to the floor and make for the coast on the flat and straight asphalt road, not having any clue what those kilometres-per-hour signs really mean.

There's no traffic coming from any direction anyway, and along with the knowledge of this being off season, I think that I'm going to be okay.

Though I am packing a pistol in my beach bag, which probably should give me a little pause for thought.

It doesn't, though.

Before I know it, I can feel those cobblestones rocking my buttocks again, like a knobbly fingered massage, and I can see the sea opening up ahead of me. The pebbles glistening in the late-morning sun, the seaweed banked up on some of the rocks further away.

And, the best part, not a soul in sight.

Except for the barman at *Por La Playa*, of course.

Once I've parked up, I make for what's becoming my regular's stool at the beach hut, and I smile at the black, moustached barman, trying to elicit some sort of response from him: for good or ill.

No dice.

"Señora?" he says, without looking up from his mounted glasses.

"The usual."

He gives me a slight nod and then digs out one of his glasses. I notice that it looks a little dusty, probably from the dirt blowing in over the hills on the wind.

He gives it a puff of breath and then shines it up with his manky cloth, before running it beneath his tap and giving it a proper clean out.

I guess it's good to know that all the fundamental rules of hygiene are being adhered to here.

He does me that same drink as before. Lime juice and fizzy water. This time he doesn't try to dose me up with any rum or whatever it was that he tried to dose it with before.

With all that done, the drink served to me, I simply rock back on my stool and feel the sun beating against my cheeks, beating down on my neck. Giving me a thorough roasting.

It's only when I've finished my first drink that the barman actually makes proper eye contact with me, a hinting gaze rather than all the avoiding and turning away he's been trying to do. Now I can see that he has quite nice, hazel eyes, just on the brink of being green. But not quite there.

I wonder if this is my opportunity to make conversation with him, but, what do you know, he beats me to the punch.

He holds his hand up to his face, knuckles outwards, and I see the pink flesh about the edges of his fingers. "Be careful," he says, and then points upwards, to the sky. "The sun."

I nod to him, fix a smile on my lips, and wonder, because of the warm feeling that's thrumming through me, whether or not he might've slipped a little something in my drink.

I bend down, reach to my beach bag which sits beneath my stool, fumble about inside there, and then draw out a wide-brimmed, straw sunhat. One of those ones that I've always thought would be good for gardening.

If I ever got good at gardening.

If everything I tried to plant or water or *nurture* in some way wouldn't just turn to crispy brown dust.

Maybe gardening is my true calling and I just don't know it yet.

Yeah, and maybe those bosomy fifty-something ladies on those gardening TV shows are just *made* for the life of an assassin.

With the hat plonked down over my head, and the strain of the sun no longer a factor on my skin, no longer beating down on me, I look back to the barman.

But he's already busying himself with his glasses again. Polishing them with that cloth of his, and thinking of who knows what.

As I suck myself to the bottom of my next glass of fizzy water and lime juice, I decide that, since I'm on holiday, I might as well push the boat out.

Pretend for once in my life that I'm not a borderline sociopathic Londoner.

"Had this bar long?" I say.

The barman flinches. Looks towards me, eyes wide and very white. "Huh?" he says.

I decide to take a leaf out of his book, and I point to the beach hut, to the roof of dried rushes. "This bar? Have you had it a long time?"

He studies me for several seconds. Lines of wrinkles seem to sprout about his eyes. "Yes," he says, and then looks down, down at the glass he's currently cleaning to a polish . . . I guess to make a slicker landing surface for the dirt.

He seems quite keen to end the conversation there, but I'm determined not to make a waste of my attempted discourse.

It's not easy to make conversation with strangers.

Not for me anyway.

"Is it much busier here in the summer months?"

This time he doesn't even bother to glance up. "Yes. Much busy." Then his eyes swivel from side to side, as if looking for something else to take his attention, and then, apparently finding nothing, his eyes find mine. "You must take care."

A slight shudder flows through my nerves. But I brush it off, reminding myself that I'm packing *Solecito* right down at my ankles if I need it. "And why's that?" I say, trying to keep my tone, my expression, neutral.

He shakes his head, and tries to brush me off. But I'm not having any of it.

If there's one thing I can't stand—*truly* can't stand—it's when someone dances about a topic, poking at it, but never wanting to bring it to the surface.

Well, I'm determined that he *is* going to bring it to the surface.

"Why is it?" I say, this time my tone harder.

He glances up at me, and then looks over the beach, back to the road which leads up and out of San Floriano. "You know why."

"No, I don't."

He nods, completes his scan of the horizon, for whatever thing he's looking for, and then he turns back to me. Meets me with those beautiful, almost mournful eyes of his and says, "Yes. You do."

* * *

There's nothing else notable about our conversation after that ominous jab, and we only speak again when I lay down the euros for my drinks: three in all.

And then I head down to the beach, spread out my towel, and set up my camp.

I didn't bring a book, not even my mobile, which is still very much switched off and stashed away in my bedside table.

Today I just want to spread myself out and lull myself into a sun-soaked sleep.

It feels like I really need it.

And so I set myself up on some larger stones, and make a fairly comfortable bed with the bath towel. Just as I settle down I see a crab scuttle out from beneath the dank shade of the bluish rocks, and make off in the direction of the sea.

Crabs too, for me, count as creepy-crawlies, so I do feel a slight quiver through my blood, and a chill enter my heart.

But I tell myself that, most likely, that's a lonely crab. And he's wandering off to the sea to maybe go and find a friend. There're *certainly* no more crabs lurking beneath these rocks. And *none* of them have sharpened-up pincers ready to give me a good pinching.

I guess that I've been lying here, on these rocks, listening to the tide sweep in and out, the rocks skitter up in the water before being dumped back down, for what seems like an hour or more.

At least that's what my stomach's telling me. It's grumbling away asking just where lunch is coming from.

And it's a good question. Because, as I lie there, eyes clasped shut, straw hat draped down over my face, I do a mental sweep of San Floriano, realise that I haven't seen any restaurants, nothing like that sort of thing. And I doubt that the patron of *Por La Playa* will be pleased to see me back there, let alone ordering food that I'm one-hundred-per-cent certain does not get cooked up in his beach hut.

I'm halfway decided just to sit this lunch out, lie here on the beach for the rest of the afternoon, and let my stomach do its grumbling sideshow and whatever, when, for some reason, I feel like someone's watching me.

It's like a tingle right to my bones. And all the other sounds, the wash of the tide, and the gentle, distant squawking of birds, seem to dip out for a moment or two.

I whip my hat off my face, bring it down to my chest, and when I look up, back up to San Floriano, I see the van.

Germo's van.

And Germo himself, dressed in his suit, green-tinted sunglasses, arms folded across his chest. Clearly staring right at me.

The wash of saliva in my mouth, from the hunger pangs announcing themselves all over my stomach, becomes a secondary thought, and I sit up straight, and stare right back at him.

For several moments he just stands there. Still looking. Apparently unmoved.

Maybe it's the sea breeze blowing cold all of a sudden, or the stench of salt suddenly becoming thick in the air, or, more than likely, the heat of the sun finally going to my brain, but I rush up onto my feet, and I make a skittling beeline for Germo.

Him, though, cool as anything—*cool* as he has been the whole time since I first set eyes on him—simply turns on his heel, un-latches the driver's door, and steps inside.

I'm only at the base of the steps which lead back up to the promenade when I hear that distinctive, grizzly-bear growl of the van's engine starting up, and I know that there's not a chance of me being able to catch him now.

Sure enough, I get to the top of the steps, clutching the rusted-up metal banister, to see the backside of the van disappearing off up the slope and out of San Floriano.

I cast a glance back to *Por La Playa*, see the barman staring back out at me, shining up one of those glasses with his cloth still. He gives me the slightest of nods, and then disappears off into the depths of his hut.

And I'm all alone again.

The whole thing gets me so riled up that I almost forget my beach bag. Forget about the gun nestled inside of it.

Almost, but not quite.

CHAPTER TWELVE

The other thing about holiday time is that it doesn't just make confusion of all the days, it chews up time itself too.

I can hardly believe what I'm doing when I sit myself down on those broad stone steps of Brian's mansion, again wearing my naughty little black number—black plimsolls—and feeling the dusty wind blow against my cheeks.

Beside me I have my handbag all packed, *Solecito* all on board, of course. It'd be mighty naïve of me to set out for this meeting, with a reputation like mine, without something little and nasty.

. . . Well, not so little.

Over the past few days I've felt the weather turning. At night a chill has crept into the air. A real bite. There seems to be more dust carrying on the winds, and though it's a warm wind, it seems to dirty everything. I'm sure that the whiteness of the mansion has become dulled over the past few days with the constant lashing of the wind.

Whenever I breathe in it seems like I breathe in equal amounts dust and air. And it's like I've got sandpaper at the back of my throat.

And I've also noticed the days have become cloudier, overcast.

Today is the most overcast of them all, though. And contrary to what the girl said to me out there in the middle of nowhere, it's looking far more likely I'm going to get a soaking than catch a sunstroke.

I really haven't packed for that. Just about the most weatherproof thing I've brought with me is my skin, and even with the state of these clouds looming overhead, I bet my internal organs are at least keeping half an eye out in case they get wet.

The strangest thing is the deathly silence all around the mansion. It makes my footsteps louder, almost makes them ring about me. The bugs don't make any sound. I guess they've made other plans, gone to see their families while this coming storm blows itself out, or something.

Another thing I've noticed is just how I don't feel much like eating or drinking anything at all. But I reckon that might be more down to the coming event rather than the weather's fault . . . though maybe that's the Londoner in me coming out again, wanting to blame the weather for everything.

In truth, I feel like a schoolgirl about to head off to her friend's house for the day. And that's what it's like . . . kind of. Me, eager and sitting here, getting a numb bottom from these cool stone steps, and staring off into the distance, watching for the approaching car.

Except I'm *not* eager, and certainly *not* looking forwards to *any-thing* about today.

She said that I might get some sort of kick out of the culture.

What kick do I want to get out of seeing an animal being killed for enjoyment?

Killing is *never* for enjoyment. It's a cool and horrid business. And a necessary one too.

The very idea of bullfighting, of this cheapening of death, of turning it into some sort of a spectacle, with its well-embroidered uniforms, and pre-historic killing tools.

That's no way to take care of any living being.

Humans included.

Well, just look at this: Anna Harris the Moralist.

In the end, I do spot the rising dust in the distance, see the van as it trucks along, apparently totally oblivious of those steep slopes that fall away at the side of the dirt path.

And I wait for the exact moment that I can see Germo's face peering out from beneath the windscreen.

Those green-tinted sunglasses. The suit. The empty expression.

One thing's for certain, today he has some answers to dish out.

Or else.

∗ ∗ ∗

The van comes to a halt with a *scrunch* of gravel as all its brake pads get hammered right at the same time. I'm sure that I can smell a slight bitter scent of burning rubber. But it's not enough to distract me from how pissed off I am about that business back at the beach.

And his *voyeurism* back there.

I watch as he leans across the dashboard, unlatches the passenger door, and I watch the door creak open on its hinge. The seat just waiting for me to occupy it.

The new-car smell is so strong today that it almost competes with the dust carrying on the breeze.

Almost.

He faces forwards, hands on the wheel, lips pressed tightly together, as I clamber in and buckle myself up.

I've hardly had a chance to close the door behind me before he hits the accelerator, sends the car reeling off in a spin of wheels and a snarl of engine.

I feel the gentle caress of the ventilators' stale air up against my face, smudging the sweat all over my skin.

As he navigates the dirt path, I put the drop alongside us out of my mind . . . *somehow* . . . and I turn to him, voice firm and hard, and hand buried within my handbag, ready to pull out *Solecito* if required.

"Just what the hell were you doing, at the beach?"

He drives on. Hands gripping the wheel. Staring ahead.

Unshakable.

Unmoveable.

In a minute, if he doesn't answer my question, I'm going to test whether or not he's *unkillable*.

I wait till we've got to the end of the dirt track, and then I say, "Stop the car."

He ignores me. Glances right. Then left. And then pulls out onto the asphalt main road.

My words get soaked up by the roaring engine and the *hum* of the tyres as they power along the flat surface, as if they're *pleased* to have finally found the asphalt.

This time I really give it some wellie. Not taking any chances that I won't be heard . . . that I'll be *misunderstood*.

"Stop!"

A brief pause. Car keeps going forwards. Germo remains detached. Unmoved totally by me. And then, with the slightest of motions, he swerves over to the side of the road. Kills the speed. I listen to the pebbles as they ping up against the paintwork.

And then, all at once, we're stopped.

He switches off the ignition. I can hear his breathing. See the gentle rise and fall of his chest. Of those lumped-up pecs through his shirt.

Today he's wearing a tie. A black tie. And it hangs down to his belt buckle. It flops gently with the motion of his breathing.

I can feel myself tingling all over. Blood rushing to my cheeks. My hand, almost unconsciously, working at the zip of my handbag.

And it's then when he whips out his hand. Catches my wrist with his meaty, sausage-like fingers, and squeezes hard till I'm forced to release the zip, and peer back at him.

Into those grey eyes.

Like always, his expression is neutral. Today he has dark bags beneath his eyes. Almost like fledgling bruises. And I can smell his cologne, thick in my nostrils: that *masculine* musky stench, with a slight hint of cranberry.

The wind blows against the side of the parked-up van and I wonder if we're going to sit here all day, just like this. Me staring into his eyes. And him staring into mine.

Him holding my wrist in that vicelike grip of his.

I can feel the blood throbbing up where he holds my wrist, and I want to tell him to let go, but I guess that he's not all that inclined to do so.

Once someone's put a gun to your head, it certainly doesn't do wonders for your trust in said person. If I was him, I wouldn't trust me.

But that's not it. I know that.

And it's only as I notice him bending into me, those grey eyes becoming all-consuming in my vision, and his thirsty lips pressing hard against mine that I realise he's not worried about the gun at all.

Or, at least, that wasn't the reason he grabbed hold of me.

It's because he *wants* me.

* * *

His tongue wades into my mouth. Velvety and smooth. Nothing like the appearance he shows the rest of the world. And it's warm in that mouth. And I feel myself exploring too. Pushing him back. My fingers spreading themselves across that divine chest, as if giving those pecs a test run.

I feel his heart pounding. And the warmth pouring out through his skin. And I can feel all the pent-up tension in his muscles, all hard-coiled like sprung wire, and I can only dream of getting to see those without niggly clothes getting in the way.

The only thing that stops us taking this any further, or perhaps pulling a swift U-turn and fleeing back to the mansion, is the rumble of Germo's mobile. Down in the space beneath the handbrake. It rumbles across the knobbly plastic surface.

When Germo draws back from me, he wears a faint smile, and that same sparkle I noticed in those grey eyes of his is back. Glimmering in the overcast daylight that bounces in through the windscreen.

He lets loose a slight exhale, and then snatches his mobile up, presses it to his ear and says, "Si?"

I listen to the garbled voice on the other end. But, even if the speaker was loud enough, it's speaking in Spanish.

As it turns out, from where I sit on the edge of this conversation, Germo is just about as mute as he is in English. He says nothing, just listening in to that incessant babble before barking a final, "Si," and hanging up.

He replaces the mobile back down in its space beneath the handbrake. Casts a glance back over to me. He's not smiling now. And that sparkle has gone from his eyes.

"Do we have to get a move on?" I say, feeling somewhat woozy, kind of like chocolate fondue all through my insides.

". . . Yes."

In that same mood, I find myself clapping my hands together, letting out a girlish giggle. "It speaks," I say. "Isn't that remarkable?"

He says nothing as he turns the ignition, purses his lips, and then pulls back out onto the road.

I watch him in profile, see that he has a slight twitch in his right eye—the one which I can see from here—and I know that his boss is getting anxious about timings.

Maybe he's had his suspicions of Germo, thought that he might've been more than a *little* interested in me.

Funny thing is, until right now, till he planted that sweet, Latin-blooded kiss on me, I had no idea how I really felt about it.

But, all things considered, he does have a terrific body. And he does have a certain attitude about him.

And I always did like my men seen and not heard.

CHAPTER THIRTEEN

Germo seems to be in a hurry all of a sudden. He has his foot pressed to the floor and our surroundings, mostly orange-red dirt, with the occasional boulder thrown in for variation, blur past the windows.

It's a good thing the road's straight, and that there's really no steering to be done. Because I've got the feeling that even someone as strongly built as Germo would struggle to stop this speeding van in a hurry.

The first raindrop falls all fat and splatters itself near enough across the entire width of the windscreen. Then another drops. And another. Before I know it, we're stuck in the middle of an downpour so heavy that it's almost like a thick mist surrounding us on all sides.

The drop in temperature is almost instant. I feel a chill pass round the neck of my dress, bring my skin out into goose bumps. I bring my arms up to my chest for warmth, try a little rubbing there—an old Army trick—but it doesn't do all that much for me.

I still have the honey-like taste of Germo's tongue in my mouth, and his cologne, with that odd, but quite alluring, hint of cranberry sends tingles passing through me.

The rain hammers down on the asphalt, seeming to form instant lakes about us. The wheels of the car slosh through the standing water, sending it spraying up.

When I look off back over my shoulder, out through the rear window, I can't see the road behind us. Just mounted, dark-bottomed clouds pressing down. And rain streaking the air all the way off to the horizon.

"Bullfight off?" I say.

Germo mumbles something under his breath and keeps his grip firmly on the steering wheel, still keeping the van barrelling forwards into the never-ending gloom.

I content myself with looking out my window, observing the perspiration all clouded up on the inside of the glass. I wipe a hole in the mist with the heel of my hand and look out across the rain-battered landscape, doing my best to see something—*anything*—out there at all.

I have to admit that I'm glad I've got a driver today. I've never been the best when it comes to driving in extreme weather.

Never been the best when it comes to driving at all, really.

We steam on like that for what I see, glancing to the green-LED-lit clock on the laminated black dashboard, is just over an hour and a half.

I guess that we've already gone past the spot where we had the meeting a while back. Almost a week ago now. It seems a long time. Seems even longer ever since Germo planted that kiss on me.

On the horizon I pick out a town rising up out of the gloom ahead, as if the asphalt road was only built to lead up to this specific spot. I look to Germo, see that he's still concentrating. He gives nothing away. It's like nothing has even happened between us at all.

He just drives, brow slightly furrowed and knuckles white on the wheel.

As we draw closer to the town, the weather eases off a little. The sky lightens up. There's no longer that driving rush of rain all around. The rain's only a steady veil now.

We pass through the outskirts of the town. All white-washed houses with dainty peach-coloured roofs. Several of them have hanging baskets: flowers of violet, and pink, and blue all bustling within them.

The asphalt road is replaced by cobblestones. And the road looks well preserved, not only all the cobblestones kept in place, no doubt replaced when they break free, but the road is so *clean*, as if someone comes in at night and buffs the cobbles up.

I see people in the streets. Strange after being isolated for such a long time … well, it feels like a long time because I'm more used to London, and being squeezed in among the—what is it?—eight or nine million now?

I watch a few of them.

Men wearing loose cotton shirts, and baggy corduroy trousers, and sturdy boots.

Women in dresses and sandaled feet, others in jeans and t-shirts.

All of them popping umbrellas, the rain streaking off the waterproof fabric, dribbling down onto the ground.

Families huddle together. The men and women combined with a scattering of children, all of them ducking and weaving, in and out, between their parents' legs.

There's a *nice* feel to this town. A sense of life here compared to the stilted feel back at the mansion, and at San Floriano.

I turn to Germo and ask, "What's this place called?"

He continues to face forwards, keeping the car slow as it rocks along the cobblestones. His eyes skitter about the crowds, obviously keeping an eye on any stray children that might get it into their heads to rush out in front of him.

Though it's just a hunch, I reckon the van will have pretty much state-of-the-art brakes, and I guess Germo can stop this great hulk dead in a matter of milliseconds.

"Gaviota," he says finally.

As we go on further, I realise that all the people are headed in a single direction. All of them pour out of side alleys. And I know that this truly is going to be a *cultural* experience.

Because I know they're all headed for the bullfight.

Like us.

* * *

The bullring soon towers above us. A great big circular building made of red brick. It's open-aired, but I think I knew that already.

As we draw closer I get the strangest feeling that I can smell blood in my nostrils. That it's just wafted right up to me. I breathe in a couple more times, not wanting to smell it again, but wanting to be sure.

Yes, that's what it smells like.

Blood.

I can taste it in my mouth, and I feel a twitch pass up my spine.

As we draw to a halt outside the periphery of the bullring, apparently headed for a car park of some sort, I can hear the gentle *babble* of the crowd.

Of all those men and woman and children on their way to see a slaughter.

Germo winds down his window with a *whine*, and I note the navy-blue uniformed policeman standing there. A baseball cap drawn low down so that from where I sit I can only make out the tip of his nose.

Germo says something or other and the policeman waves us inside, into a complex filled with nicely shining cars, cars that, even with my lack of knowledge on the subject, I know are extremely expensive.

Put it this way, I'm going to take care when I'm opening my door not to ding anyone's paintwork.

Just as he has been ever since the kiss, Germo is all business, and he brings the car to a stop in one of the yellow-painted spaces nearest to the bullring itself. Seemingly in the same gesture, he yanks the keys from the ignition, and he cracks the handle on his door.

Not having had time to get myself ready for this abrupt exit, I take a quick moment to check my face in the passenger-seat mirror, see that there's nothing too apocalyptic going on, and I slide my buns over the seat and emerge out into the concrete car park outside.

I just about keep in step with Germo as he marches his way across the car park, and over to an opening marked with the letter 'C' in white paint.

I'm about to remind him to lock the car when I hear that giveaway *toot* over my shoulder. As I walk fast after Germo, I take care to keep my handbag close. To keep it tight to my chest.

And I hope that no one's going to think of searching me on the way in.

Because I really don't think my Spanish is up to explaining just what I'm doing in possession of a handgun.

✶ ✶ ✶

As it turns out, there isn't any security, at least not on this side of the bullring, not by the area where the people in the posh cars park up in any case.

We climb the exposed concrete steps, and I take care to keep an eye on Germo's heels, pleased that I decided on plimsolls today.

High heels would've been a mistake.

We emerge up onto a floor which I guess to be only two of three below the very highest point of the bullring, and it seems like we've reached our destination since Germo is making off, hitting a hard stride once more.

I take a brief moment to take in the bullring. All laid out down below.

Not only has the rain stopped now, but the clouds have cleared. And there's none of that heaviness in the air any longer. No feeling that a thunderstorm is about to strike at a moment of its choosing. Though I guess it already has.

I can smell the wet earth carried on the air, and it tastes a little bitter at the back of my throat. As I glance about the arena, I can see people already beginning to file in, bringing that same melodic buzz of Spanish conversation along with them.

I can see the circle of orange dust in the centre, and then I look to the cement steps that serve as seats that curve all around the arena.

A little further along I see a gate which leads into the arena, and I guess that's where the bulls come from.

When I look up, I see that Germo is standing off along the corridor, in the shadow there. But I've been quite enjoying this brief spate of having the sun glowing on my skin, like it is now. I guess I wouldn't feel the same if I was dressed in a suit like Germo is.

So I shove off towards him and he keeps on his way.

We arrive to a door manned by a middle-aged woman with a green hi-vis vest. She's wearing gloves. Actually wearing gloves. And what looks to be a fairly thick coat.

As for me, I can already feel the sweat prickle at the back of my neck.

Germo has a brief conversation with her, and then she opens the door and lets us through.

We emerge into a crimson-carpeted corridor that curls around with the shape of the bullring. I watch as Germo tilts his head to one side, taking in the doors as we pass them by.

They all have names in Spanish, all done up in gilded lettering on black-laminated tags.

Apparently, he reaches the one we're looking for because he stops, gazes back at me, gives me the slightest of slight smiles . . . no more than a little curl of the mouth at either side, and then he straightens his tie, jigs the creases out of his lapels and knocks curtly twice.

I stand a little way back, maybe eight or nine paces away from him.

Only now do I notice that there are high-contrast colour photographs hung up all along the walls here. And that they depict various bullfights. All of them shots of a fight in motion.

The matador with his cape flung back, that ridiculous, carnivalesque outfit flowing in the wind, or perhaps with movement. And the bull driving its horns downwards, making for the offered scarlet cape.

I get in the subtlest of smirks before the door creaks open.

There's a rapid-fire shot of Spanish, and then I hear a familiar voice.

"Anna, *awfully* lovely to see you!"

CHAPTER FOURTEEN

The girl from before appears in the doorway, and I notice that Germo has faded into the background, in that way he's got a knack of doing.

Today she's wearing a sweet, cream dress with green flowers stamped all over it. And it makes her skin seem fairer. Makes her seem *younger* . . . if she really needed that at all.

Her sable hair tumbles down onto her shoulders, neatly sleek and those blond streaks seeming to bring out her fair skin even more.

And those rosy brown eyes just gleam over the top of everything. Always studying. All-seeing. And, most certainly, to be watched with great care.

She's wearing a lilac-like scent that puffs out over me like a cloud as she leans forwards and plants a kiss on each of my cheeks, then stands back to take me in as if we're long-lost relatives going through the motions of the first visit in decades.

This girl is hardly two decades old, for God's sake.

"Yes," she says, beaming. "Simply wonderful to see you here. I am so glad tha' you could accept the invitation. I can promise you tha' this will be a wonderful day for you. The best day in your whole time in Spain, perhaps."

I manage a smile. And it's not even that snarky. "Oh, yes, I hope so," I say.

"Please," she says, standing back, waiting for me to slip in past her.

I hesitate a moment, look to Germo, as if *he's* going to be the one to take the first step in through the door. As if *he's* the special guest here.

Another deep breath later and I'm sidling my way in past the girl.

I emerge into a box, an area of the arena cordoned off, with cover overhead, whereas, for the most part, the rest of the arena is open air. There're about a dozen or so seats all filed in here. And a division separates us from the box next door, and a mauve-coloured, well-ribboned barrier separates us from the plebs down below.

The seats here look much bulkier, and much better cushioned, than the rest of the arena. Certainly more comfortable than those concrete steps anyway.

And I think that if it wasn't for the impending bullfight, and having to suffer my way through it, I might actually quite enjoy this hospitality.

It makes some difference to pottering about the mansion all day in any case.

There's no one else here. Just me, the girl and Germo, and this enormous white-clothed table all laid out with foods: fish, and meat, and rice, and other local specialities, that are all doing a good job of making my gut wriggle.

It's funny how much of an appetite a girl can cook up from a sneaked kiss and a two-hour-long drive.

I look back out over the bullring but there's really not all that much happening down there, besides there being a few more people filed into their seats.

No sign of the bulls, or the matadors, or the whatever elses, for that matter.

Just me and the girl.

And Germo.

When I turn back to the girl she's grinning from ear to ear. No surprises there, then. I wonder if she's trying to cook up some sort of a bimbo act before slipping a knife through my ribcage . . . from the back, of course.

Maybe I should stop being so cynical.

And if the worst comes to the worst, well, at least I'm packing *Solecito*.

My little amigo.

"You look lovely," she says to me, fluttering her eyelashes in that way that debutants do, or so I'm told.

"Thanks," I say, unable not to feel the slightest of glows through me, because if there's one thing that I'm *not* immune to it's complements.

Call me vain if you like.

She takes her place at my shoulder and screws up her eyes to look out over the arena. To the bullring down below, and to the seats that're filling up at a decent rate now.

I guess that maybe the arena is approaching a quarter full, something like that.

"You mus' have lots of questions," she says, still looking below.

"You could say that."

I feel those precious, china-doll fingers of hers creep their way up my back, and then settle down on my shoulder, as if we're *pals* or something. But I don't actively try to shrug them off. After all, I'm supposed to be being a good girl today.

"When my father comes, you will know what you must do."

"I'm looking forward to it."

"Yes," she says, "it shall be an interesting offer for you."

"What's your name?"

She removes her hand from my shoulder, brings her fingers to her mouth, opened up in that ridiculous O-shape like before. "I never said, did I?"

"No."

Her features soften up a little as she shakes her head, apparently out of disbelief, but I get the impression that this is a bit of a game . . . that *all* of this so far has been a game.

"Then allow me to introduce myself," she says, holding out her hand to me.

I take it in mine. Just as fragile as I'd thought. I could probably break the bones if I squeeze just a little too hard.

"My name is Viviana."

* * *

I take a seat alongside Viviana, on the front row of our box. The barrier with its mauve ribbon is about up to my chest height. Just high enough so I don't need to see the people sitting in front of me. But not quite high enough to block out the sight of the rest of the arena.

The Great Unwashed.

I suppose if it was a little higher still, then I wouldn't be able to see the bullring down below either. And that, really, would be a travesty.

As the bullring fills up even more, now well over three quarters of the way full, the air buzzes with chatter. Everyone seeming to speak right at the same time.

I look over the faces, look down at the families. See those bronzed faces, and the hampers they all carry between them. Sharing out food among themselves. Squash for the children, and wine among the grownups.

It makes me pine a little for my own family. For my kids: Ben and Josie, the two of them seem such a long way away right now. Off there in Blighty, getting rained on, frozen up, and the rest.

I guess I haven't had the weather all my own way what with the showers and overcast conditions of the last day or so.

Brightening up now, though.

In fact it's a fairly glorious afternoon of sun beaming down on the bullring, down on the spectators, baking the dirt.

Something's going on down there in the bullring now, some people in garishly coloured costumes are emerging out onto the dirt. I'm not that conscious of it, but I suppose it's my sidelong glance to Viviana that prompts her to give me an explanation.

"The toreros: the picadors, on the horses, with the silver thread, and the banderilleros with the flags. And the matador, he is the one with the gold thread. But I think you know about him. They are going on parade. Before they commence the fight."

They all look just about as ridiculous as one another in their sequined uniforms, all bright colours, and those oddly shaped hats they wear on their heads, and that make me think of admirals.

"And the bulls?" I say, doing my best not to sound flippant.

"That is after."

I focus down on the arena, watch the two men mounted on the horses bobbing in the saddle as they do a sweep, as they wave to the assembled masses: to the men, women and children, who wave back to them, some of them with sandwiches or plastic cups in their hands.

"And your father?" I say.

Viviana continues to stare down at the bullring and I see a little colour enter her cheeks. I wonder if I've embarrassed her in some way but write that off as me being too sensitive.

What right does *she* have?

I mean, she's the one that's dragged me here, somewhere I *really* don't want to be.

She's the one that claims she has a proposal for me . . . that claims that her *father* has a proposal for me.

"He should arrive soon," she says, but her voice is quiet, almost down to a whisper.

I chance a glance back over my shoulder, back to Germo.

He stands up there, shades fixed across the bridge of his nose, his hands folded, one on top of the other, resting on his belt buckle.

He looks all business.

And I quite like it.

I turn back to Viviana. "Well, you must be someone important to have someone like that looking out for you, you know, a bodyguard?"

Viviana flinches at the word 'bodyguard' for some reason. I wonder why. She's almost recovered her fair complexion from before, managed to get shot of that unsightly flush in her cheeks, and she tries to brush off her flinch with a gentle smile at me, even managing to linger in my gaze for a few seconds.

"Yes," she says, "I must be careful. That is the reason why."

"And why's that exactly?"

She pouts, and then busies herself with the mauve ribbon which hangs off the front of the box. She reminds me a little of an obstinate child, ignoring the authority of an unfamiliar adult. "I cannot say."

"Why?"

Her Adam's apple bobs a little in her throat, and when she speaks again her voice is louder, and her tone much frostier. "Because my father has forbidden it."

"I see," I say, turning my attention back down to the bullring, where the garishly dressed men seem to be filing their way back into the open gate.

And I guess, soon, I'm going to get to see my first bull slaughtered.

* * *

I can't take my eyes off the bullring as a pair of men bring a bull, stamping and snorting, out from the shady entrance to the ring.

The crowd all around me gives a cheer, and it clashes with the icy feeling ripping through my gut. With the vague taste of vomit in my mouth, and the spiralling sensation of nausea creeping in.

Maybe it's the effect of the sun beating down on me, the roof over our heads doesn't cover the front rows of the seats in this cordoned-off area.

I forgot to bring my straw hat today, didn't think it would be necessary, and even now, what must be around three or four o'clock in the afternoon, the sun is cooking my brain like a steak, frying my eyes like eggs.

I look to the matador, the one who stands on the dirt, with a scarlet cape draped over his arm, and a sword held down at his side, its edge gleaming gold in the sunlight.

What's the matter with me?

What sort of person has no problem with snuffing a human life out, and then cries their eyes out over a bull . . . an *animal?*

It's not like I'm a vegetarian either. Far from it. But, I guess, I never get to see my meat being put to the sword. Not like this. Not with the sole intention of causing pain.

That's not the right way to bring about death.

What sort of person am I?

Am I immoral?

Or morally reprehensible?

How can I kill so coldly, and so quickly, without batting an eyelid?

. . . Or, at least, I used to be able to. Before I used to be able to zone out. To flip my Kill Switch and next thing I'd know the thing was done. The money in my account.

But then the nightmares came.

Ever since Elizabeth Newman.

And they've not ceased since.

Over the kafuffle from the crowd down below, I hear the creak of the hinges on the door to the box. Someone entering. Coming in.

Only when I turn to look over my shoulder do I remember just what I'm doing here. What I'm *supposed* to be doing here.

That's right.

I was waiting for RP.

And here he is.

CHAPTER FIFTEEN

R P, it turns out, has lush brown hair with only a couple of sashes of grey, which comes down to the cusp of his neck. And he has a wrinkled, tanned complexion. So much browner than Viviana's complexion that it makes me doubt whether he really is her father.

Then again, I guess that Viviana's mother could've been the fair one.

RP turns first to Germo, mutters a word to him, which Germo greets with a nod, and then he approaches me and Viviana, both of us sat there on the seats, with the bullfight right on the brink of commencing.

To be honest, I'm glad to have a good reason to turn away. And to put it out of my mind for a while, though I'm preparing myself for the *snick* of the sword, for the *slice* of flesh, and the *spurt* of blood.

But it's one thing to see it, and quite another to hear it.

And, for now, I'll take hearing over seeing.

RP wears a causal jacket over a thin-checked, blue-and-white shirt. He wears it with the top three or four buttons undone, so that it exposes his greying chest hair and, a little beneath, his tanned and slightly wrinkled chest.

I also, though I can't be certain, think I catch sight of a patch of fried skin: purple and blotchy.

A scar.

"Mrs Harris," he says, extending his hand to me, and grinning, just like his daughter, from ear to ear.

I don't think to correct him on my name right now, deciding that I'll operate a three-strikes system . . . or maybe I'll just sound him out for a while before knowing just how far I can push my liberties.

One thing I notice, as he takes my hand, is how Viviana just remains facing down into the bullring, not even a simple hello for her father on his arrival.

As I turn my attention back to RP, I see that he has noticed this, and he gives a Gallic shrug—I'm sure his daughter has learned from the best.

He glances past me, down to the bullring, where I can already hear those stomach-churning roars of the crowd, and that awful *clang* of metal on metal.

For a moment, I'm certain that he's going to force me to turn around, *make* me watch the grim spectacle playing out down below, but, instead, he shepherds me off to the table complete with the food . . . I have to admit that I'd been wondering when I'd be let loose on it . . . and he waits for me to take a plate off the pile before taking one for himself.

"Thank you for coming today, Mrs Harris, I really *do* appreciate it."

Strike Two.

I glance over at Germo who remains just as stoic—and *silent*— as ever, gazing out from beneath his sunglasses, apparently following the bullfight as it happens down below.

As I pile up the cold meats, and the crumbly pieces of bread, take more than my fair share of olives, I feel a slight flush of anger flow through me. Because I have to remind myself of the circumstances that have seen me coming today.

And now's the time to confront the *maker* of those circumstances.

So, with my plate fully loaded, and caught between a pair of mutually opposing desires: to comfort my hunger, and *not* to see the bullfight, I come to an unhappy compromise, and remain standing. Deciding to just be direct with this guy as much as I can be. "Do you think you can just tell me what this is about?"

RP smiles with half his mouth, and continues to pluck out his own snack time, cobbling together his own plate of goodies. He smells a little of elderberries, and the mint on his breath makes me wonder if he's just brushed his teeth. "Yes," he says, "I believe that is fair. I do not want to worry you unduly, of course."

"Of course," I say, my eyes wandering back towards the door, in the opposite direction to the bullring. "So what is it?"

He's apparently finished stocking his plate, so he stands before me, shoulders slightly slumped, his mouth fixed in a distant smile. "I wish to apologise if any of my attempts to approach you, Mrs Harris—"

Third strike.

"*Miss* Harris," I say, correcting him.

He smiles even wider. "Yes, *Miss* Harris, I would like to say how sorry I am if I have made you feel at all uncomfortable at a time that I am sure is supposed to be for relaxation. You have come here, to my country, to spend your holiday, and so why should I intrude, eh?"

Precisely my point, I think to myself, but I keep schtum.

"I wanted to wait, to *earn* your trust before I made you our proposal, and that was why I had the package sent, so that you would know how serious I am." His features crinkle just a little and his rosy brown eyes—the same as his daughter's—seem to ember away. "Did you like my gift to you? Have you brought it with you today?"

I think over my answer with extreme care, and then come to the conclusion that, really, there's no reason that I should lie to him. He could probably order Germo to give me a shakedown if he wanted, and there would most likely be nothing I could do about it.

"Yes," I say, "I brought it."

He nods. "Hmm, yes, that was as I expected."

"Sorry to be so predictable, but a girl gets a little suspicious, you know, when there's this big guy with bustling muscles following her all around the place."

I think for a second of adding that Germo spied on me at the beach, at San Floriano, but I stop short, realising that I've probably nulled whatever I held against him with that extremely mutual kiss in the car on the way over here.

"You know," I continue, "showing up in the mansion, just popping up out of *nowhere* like that?"

RP nods along, apparently sympathetic, and then, one hand still clinging to his plate, he holds the other palm outwards, as if making a reasonable argument. "But you had a gun. You could have shot him?"

I don't answer that because I know he's right . . . and, to be frank, I'm a little embarrassed about having been caught without a gun nearby for that specific encounter, though I believe I made more than amends for it in the car later on, what with all that holding the gun to Germo's temple.

RP's tone lightens, and then he says, "And what do you think? What do you think about," and his voice depends as he slips into Spanish, "*Solecito?*"

I feel my heart thrumming in my chest, but I fight it down. I realise that I've left my handbag down at the foot of my seat, down beside Viviana. But I'm hardly going to *shoot* this guy here among all these people anyway.

My mind just goes totally blank. I feel ditzy all of a sudden. Maybe it's the heat or blood being spilled by that poor innocent bull . . . or something like that. "I . . . I . . . yes, thank you," I finally settle on.

He smiles. "Excellent, that is a wonderful thing. I wanted you to feel safe. That was imperative for me before I could ask you the question."

"And what is the question?"

"Hmm," he says as he glances down at his plate of food. "We eat first, yes? And then we speak about the proposal, about what I have to ask of you."

I realise that I'm most likely not going to be able to put this off any further, and that, if I want to satisfy my hunger I'll *have* to see the bullfight . . . at least a little.

And so I flash a quick glance over at Germo, and then follow RP's lead.

∗ ∗ ∗

The dirt. The grunts. The ripple of muscles. The bull's white, foaming mouth.

But, most of all, it's the blood.

That's what does it for me.

The blood.

While sitting beside RP, with Viviana over on the other side of him, I do my best to just keep my gaze downwards, concentrated down on my plate of food. That's a good distraction. That means that I don't have to look up.

And though the food tastes of dried skin in my mouth, and I have to force myself to swallow, my stomach seems to be thanking me for finally showing it some mercy.

Now, though, now that I've finished, there's really no other place I can look other than the bullring down below, to that poor stampeding beast as it sheds its blood over the dirt, its head desperately dipping and rising in defiance.

RP explained to me that one of the most important components of a bullfight is the surprise. In bullfights, in *real* bullfights, the bull has never seen the ring before. He has never fought before. And therein lies the entertainment, because the audience witnesses the bull's shock and surprise at being found in this pitched battle to the death.

The bull acts on instinct, he follows the wave of the matador's cape, bowing his head and rushing him.

And I find myself willing, almost mouthing the words, wishing for the bull to take the matador down.

For the bull to *gore* him right through the chest.

To *kill* him.

And that makes me wonder just what this says about me, because who else am I but the matador? Cruel, trained, and deadly. Taking another creature into my own habitat, changing all the rules.

And then . . . and *then*, striking the final, killing blow.

The bull pants hard now. His legs are slightly bowed and he stumbles from side to side.

But he keeps on fighting.

Just pure, brute force shining through.

Something deep in his nature will not allow him to stop his resistance. Stubbornness.

I can feel the food in my stomach churning all around, and despite the warm air I feel my blood running boiling hot one moment and then icy cold the next.

When I glance around RP and to Viviana, I see that she is watching this. She has been watching all this happen the entire time from behind her large, oval-shaped sunglasses: the kind that seem to occupy a whole face.

But her lips are pursed, and I'm certain she is watching.

The fight finally reaches its conclusion. And I force myself to watch. To watch the blade of the sword as the matador runs the bull through. Severs some artery. Or, for all I know about the anatomy of a bull, he strikes him right through the heart.

The bull gives his final sigh and then dies.

His body pounds onto the dry earth, sending up a plume of dust.

The audience cries out in delight. The matador reaches in and withdraws the half-buried sword, raises it up to the sky, its blade soaked with blood.

RP leans into me and says, "A good fight, a *very* clean kill."

I don't think that I can possibly say that there was anything *clean* about what I've just witnessed, so I keep quiet. I'll have to remain fairly civil till I find out just what RP's after . . . and what *I* have at stake in it.

Soon after, the bullring is alive with various attendants. All of them dressed in their garish uniforms, and I turn away. I look to RP, and say, "So what is this proposal of yours?"

For the first time in our meeting, RP seems a little stuck for words, as if now that the time has come for action, for all the cards to be laid on the table, he's completely unable to follow it through.

If that's the case then I'll head off right now. Snatch up my handbag, and good, old trusty *Solecito* nestled inside, and I'll escape the mansion. Go off somewhere I can *really* have some peace. Some time to myself.

And not mess about with small-time crooks because, surely, that's just what RP is.

RP reaches up to his face, and he peels off the blue-tinted sunglasses that he's been wearing for the duration of the fight. He tucks them into the top pocket of his jacket and fixes me with a pout . . . just like one of his daughter's pouts. "Please," he says, "my name is Randolfo Perez, that is my *true* name."

RP, I think to myself. Well, even if he's not telling the truth then at least he's being consistent . . . which can sometimes be a lot to ask of the *lower* criminal elements.

"And my daughter, Viviana Perez."

"Yes," I say, feeling a touch of impatience making itself felt, "we've already met."

He strikes another pout, this time a more *profound* pout, and he raises his hand up to his chin, lays his fingers in the dimple there. "I know Brian Mathewson well, you could say that we are *partners* of a kind."

Though I'm a little reluctant to admit it, RP . . . Randolfo, has succeeded in grabbing hold of my attention for the first time today. Of course I know that he has some sort of a connection to Brian, but up until now it's just been pure speculation.

For all I knew, Germo might simply have been working for *both* Brian and this Randolfo character. Goons might be hard to come by in this particular part of the country.

Though an extremely attractive goon he might be.

"Go on," I say.

"I have heard many things about you, Anna Harris—"

"Just Anna is fine."

"Anna, I have heard a lot of things from Brian about you, and about how you are tough, and how you *always* get the job done."

I wonder if this is going to be the moment when he'll lay out the hit.

Then, at the very least, I guess I'll find out just how professional he is.

Because no *real* businessman worth his salt would call a hit on someone in such a public place as this . . . he hasn't even checked me for bugs, though I guess it's conceivable he's had the box checked.

I feel a hole opening up in my chest, that sensation I've been feeling more than a little lately. There's no other way to describe it other than feeling empty. Deeply and profoundly empty.

Of a conscience.

Of a soul.

Of everything.

But now's not the time to start blabbing away. If I can help it, I won't show him my fragile mental state, won't reveal to him that my Kill Switch is out of order.

I turn my attention back down to the bullring. The wind catches and whirls a cloud of dust, makes a mini-tornado of it, and twizzles it about for a while in the blood-soaked dirt.

My mouth is numb. I can't taste anything. And all I can smell is the blood on the air.

Though all around me people are chatting animatedly, people are laughing and having fun, I can't bring myself to share anything of their jubilation.

It feels like I am stranded on my own and very lonely island.

Left here, washed up by the tide.

Left in pieces.

I dial my concentration back into what Randolfo has to say, meeting his eyes with my own, those rosy brown eyes he shares with his daughter.

"Anna, my proposal is quite simple, I would like you to teach Viviana everything you know."

Well, think it's safe to say I wasn't expecting that.

CHAPTER SIXTEEN

'm not sure what to expect on the ride back home . . . to what I suppose *qualifies* as 'home' out here.

I managed to swindle my way out of the next couple of bull-fights that Randolfo claimed were about the happen, told him that I'd spent a little too long in the sun.

And he seemed to go for it.

The engine hums lightly, and I zone out, watching the asphalt road sweep beneath the might of the van, and I glance to Germo, take him in in profile.

I wonder if he's finally going to break out of this catharsis, or whatever it is that consists of his professional 'bruiser' image, and if he's suddenly going to proposition me in some romantic, direct way.

Recite some Spanish poetry, that sort of thing.

I bet it works on all the other female tourists.

Only difference being, I'm willing to wager that the majority of those *others* aren't killers. Or didn't *used to be* killers.

But no, it's as quiet of a journey as the one out from the mansion.

I press my head up against the chilly windowpane watching the sun glowing on the horizon, preparing to dunk itself down for the night.

Some of my senses have returned to me now. I have some aftertaste of something fishy, though I don't remember eating fish, and I can smell the rich scent of Germo's cologne, what with its sharp trace of cranberry.

I just listen to the tyres whirr their way along the road surface, every so often crunching over a piece of grit or gravel, sending it pinging off in our wake.

I have no idea what I'm going to tell Randolfo, whether or not I'll accept his offer.

Oh, sure, he has a lot of money, an absolute *ton* actually.

And he doesn't seem that shy about flashing it either, since he shoved this whole fistful of euro notes at me, 'as an advance,' when we wished one another goodbye back at the bullring.

I do wonder just how Viviana feels about this fledgling agreement since, after her father made me the offer, she really had nothing at all to say to me. She only gave me a slight smile when I said goodbye to her, and added no words at all.

Sure, I already have a ton of money saved up in the bank, a cool half a million pounds. Just sitting there and waiting for me to do something with.

But I know, in reality, that's just not going to be enough.

Not if I'm going to get away from all of this.

If I want to *start again*.

With the money that Randolfo is willing to put up for these . . . well, I suppose you could call them 'classes,' I'll more than double what I've already got.

I'll be a millionairess.

Have enough to buy a bigger house, or to buy a house that I can rent out and live off that.

Wouldn't that be a quaint way to live?

I suppose at least that way I'd just be living off the blood and sweat of the living, rather than the blood and sweat of the dead.

I suppose, in this life, that's a choice that everyone has to make at some point, and for me, in my position, that choice is just a touch starker.

Black or white.

No grey at all.

I don't even realise how close we are to being home till Germo flips the indicator, and it ticks away, an amber light flashing on the dashboard.

He rolls us back along the dirt path, going much slower this time, apparently not so rushed as he was to get us to the bullring, and why should he be, I've got no place to be and no time to be there either.

I listen for the slowing of the engine, and the *crunch* of the tyres over the dirt road as he brings us to a stop outside the mansion. At the base of those stone steps which lead up to the hefty oak front doors.

And then we just sit.

Engine idling. Ventilator ducts spewing out tepid air. And my heart throbbing away somewhere at the base of my ribcage.

Only when I feel that same familiar prickle, that feeling of someone *watching* me, do I think to turn in my seat and look over at Germo.

Of course he's staring right at me. Those grey eyes of his like a liquid, constantly shifting about, changing on me. But they hold still. Just for a second.

"The boss ask if I stay."

Despite everything that's happened today, despite that hulking, *bleeding* mass of bull I watched dying in the dirt, I can't help but raise a smile. "Is that the most you've ever said?"

He smirks. "Maybe in English."

* * *

And so I invite him in, of course, it'd be rude not to. It seems like my prospective employer, Randolfo, has given me all the reason in the world to go ahead with this act of reckless lovemaking.

Though Germo has all the muscles in the world, he's a pretty tender lover, all things considered. Not to mention all that Latino blood that must be rushing through his system twenty-four hours a day.

Times like this make me glad to have the whole mansion to myself—my *own* mansion to bring men back to.

We do it in the kitchen. In the front hall. In the sitting room, though that shady reflection of the plasma TV—let alone the possibility of being irradiated—sends me lugging him up the stairs for the final act, up to the master bedroom.

When he wanders into the bedroom, behind me, I notice those grey eyes of his gaping in a kind of childish wonder. And that childlike look to him is made all the more noticeable from his nakedness too . . . from the rippling, tanned muscles at his thighs, and that downy, blond tuft of hair—just like the hair on his head—above his box of jewels.

. . . Yes, I did just say 'box of jewels' to myself. I guess that all this alone time has finally got to me, or maybe the sun has fried my brain into a tender steak.

I'm sure that he's seen rooms as sumptuous as this one before, though, because, to me, Randolfo doesn't appear to be a man who skimps on luxury. And, if Germo has *anything* at all to do with Brian—the very fact that he's *trusted* by Brian—means that he must've experienced luxury like this before.

And so, many hours later, though with no clock in the master bedroom, and no intention of flipping on my mobile, there's no way to tell, I roll off him and onto my side. The silk sheets stick to me from all the sweating I've been doing.

It's only then that I realise how sticky it is in the room, despite the fact that night has fallen outside long ago, and the room is steeped only in moonlight.

So I pick my way across the marble floor, which at present feels so cold that it might as well be packed ice, and I reach the doors to the balcony, unlatching them and then flinging them open with a single—and, *I* think—fairly expert motion.

I pause a moment, listening in to the bugs chirping outside. And the slight, warm wind blowing its way through the long grasses and the parched ground, gathering up dust and sweeping it along. Then I turn back around and throw myself back down on the bed, like I was some sort of a giddy teenager.

I guess, in a way, I just never grew up.

Not completely, anyway.

Germo lies on his back, naked. His hands clutched together over the slight bulge of his belly. I wonder what he'll be like in twenty years or so, and then, a second later, I wipe that record from my mind, not wanting to think of it.

For me, I'm determined, he'll always be stamped in my mind as this rugged, Spanish hunk. All muscles and silence and sweat.

That salty taste of his sweat still lingers in my mouth. The smell of him too, that overwhelming odour of cologne, that sharp tang of cranberry. And I feel his warmth still oozing out onto my skin, and I relish it.

I watch him in profile for a while, watch his eyes as they blink up through the gloom, as if fascinated by some aspect of the roof above our heads . . . though it's clearly just your bog-standard, white-washed ceiling.

When he speaks, it catches me a little off guard, as if I wasn't expecting him to speak at all. And, in a way, I feel a little disappointed that he's broken the almost complete silence.

But it's not like he's some escort . . . or, at least, not *that* kind . . . and I remind myself that he *does* have permission to speak. That he's just as human as I am.

"Your gun."

He says it so softly that I ask him to repeat it, not because I didn't understand, but I almost can't comprehend how someone as bulky as he is, so rippling all over with muscles, so *powerful*, can speak that way.

He shifts over in the bed, his grey eyes staring into mine.

I have a moment's hesitation, almost as if I'm worried that he might still hold a grudge from before. That he might want to get some of his own back. But I soon ditch that assumption—again doing my best to banish Cynical Anna from my consciousness for a little while.

I reach out for my bedside table, and paw through it, feeling first my mobile—switched off, as it has been this whole time—and then I reach for the gun.

I take a hold of its grip and grab hold of it, then bring it out before me. I check the safety catch, though it's switched on . . . I might be skittish with lots of things, but never with the safety switch of my guns . . . except that time out in the hallway . . . and then, with a slight pause, I pass it into Germo's outstretched palm.

He takes hold of it. Grips it tight in his fist. And then he points it up at the roof.

I look to his eyes, to the reflection of the moonlight across them, and I see him shut one eye, and squint down the barrel as he lines up a shot, apparently in his imagination.

Then he brings the gun down and holds it up to the moonlight, reading the name on the grip. "*Solecito*," he says, and then slips me a sidelong glance. "Little sun."

"That what it means?" I say, propping myself up on my elbow, and only realising how sleepy I've got when I hear the dopey tone of my voice.

He turns his attention back to the gun, grips it tight again, and then hands it back to me.

I take it, replace it back in the drawer of the bedside table, and then shut it up.

He brings his hands back behind his head, and continues to stare up at the ceiling. I wonder if he's *trying* not to look at me . . . but that's most likely me being paranoid.

If there's one thing I've learned about myself in my years of womanhood, it's that I get all paranoid after sex. Guess it's just my thing.

And all I do to combat it this time is shut my eyes, breathe in that rich, musky scent of man, and then give a heavy exhale. When I open my eyes again, he's looking at me.

"So," he says. "What you think, uh, of the offer?"

"The offer?" I say. "To teach that little girl how to shoot a gun?" I give a little shrug. "I dunno, I'll think about it in the morning."

"Hmm," he says, turning his attention back up to the ceiling again.

I study his question. Wonder what the significance of it is. Then I remember that, as far as Randolfo is concerned, Germo is still on duty. That he's supposed to be *protecting* me . . . or perhaps that's the idea.

That same paranoia slips over me like a soggy sheet, and I think about whether he'll report in about what we've just done. It makes me wonder just *how* faithful Germo is to his boss. Not that I care. Not really. That's one of the beauties of being on holiday. Once I leave this place, leave Spain, everything'll stay here.

Unless Randolfo sees his way to coming on a visit to London, which I suppose, if he's telling the truth about being a 'partner' of Brian, isn't all that unlikely.

Still, I don't *really* care.

Another long silence stretches out between us, and I can think of only one way to break it. I mean, we've got nothing in common except for animal attraction, so what *else* are we going to do all night?

Because I certainly have no intention of sleeping.

Not till morning anyway.

CHAPTER SEVENTEEN

For some reason, when I wake up, I expect Germo to be gone. Perhaps even to have a hand-written note waiting for me on his pillow.

But, no.

He's right here still.

Lying on his side, the silk sheet just about covering the majority of his firm buttocks, his back to me as his bronzed shoulders rise and fall with his gentle breathing.

I lie still for a little while, just listening to the sounds of the house around me. To those bugs, always seeming to get up bright and early . . . though I don't suspect it's as early as I think.

The air is thick today, and the sun is shining outside. I can feel the warm wind blowing in through the wide-open balcony doors, and caressing that remaining sweat into my skin.

I'm sure that I can smell the sea carried on it too, and that gives me an idea—of what we might get up to today. It is Sunday, after all, and if Germo's *got* to work today, then the least I can do is make it pleasant for him.

I stumble up and out of bed. I'm so parched that I simply wander into the en suite, flip the tap, and then suckle at the lukewarm stream of water that flows out of it.

At the back of my mind, I'm hoping that Germo's not going to wake up at that exact moment, to see me in that posture.

I only realise I'm naked when I come back out of the en suite, and see my dressing gown—fluffy, and white, just like everything else in this house—and I shrug it on around my shoulders, flicking my hair out from the collar.

That's the thing with having sex all night, you kind of forget about the clothes.

At least I always do.

I slap my way, barefooted, along the marble floors out on the landing, and then descend down into the front hall. I stop briefly, as I always seem to do, ever since I saw that package on the dainty little table here.

I don't really know what I'm looking for.

An envelope slipped under the front doors perhaps?

But, like always, there's nothing at all there.

Just the bare, marble floors, all slicked up to a shine.

The cinnamon scent is extremely strong today. Almost strong enough to knock me out. And I wonder if it's because I was out the whole day before, that I didn't throw every last window and door in the place wide. And the mansion just ended up baking in the sun.

And that's right when I realise. When I realise that they're not only all polished up, but they're still wet. And that revelation lingers with me for another moment, my mind drawing a blank, and only understanding what it means when I shift my gaze around.

And see the cleaning lady standing there, in the doorway to the kitchen.

Blue-purple hair, brown canvas bag, and all.

Weirdly, my first thought is: *Just what's a cleaner doing working on a Sunday?*

＊ ＊ ＊

She seems just as surprised as me. Her withered fingers rising up to her purple-lipstick- painted lips, and her mouth gaping. "Oh," she says.

Either I'm getting to be bilingual, or that expression transcends both our languages . . . because that's just what I've got on my mind. Or some exclamation of surprise, in any case.

She witters something in Spanish, and though I don't have a snowball's chance in hell of understanding, for some reason I nod along, as if that'll make this all right.

When she stops speaking, I simply break out into a smile, to go with the nodding, and she smiles back at me, a little nervously, the wrinkles deepening about her mouth.

And then she takes a few steps into the front hall, onto the freshly washed-up floor, and then makes it to the door, where she rests her hand on the latch, preparing to let herself out.

Just as I'm about halfway to raising my arm, to give her a farewell wave, and to maybe push the boat out and try a tentative 'Chao', I hear the gruff and familiar voice over my shoulder.

Germo.

Well, if the cleaning lady had looked on edge before, now she looks like someone's run over her cat, or dog: depending on her personal preference. All the muscles in her body seem to firm up, and her finger joints go white from her gripping the brown canvas bag with all the cleaning goodies nestled inside.

For what seems like an hour, Germo rumbles on at her, in that sing-song voice, his Spanish, literally, going right over my head.

And she just does a lot of nodding. And, as it seems like he's wrapping up, she gives him the faintest of smiles.

She says something back to Germo for a while and then at the end she mutters something which might be 'Gracias,' but I wouldn't go on the record, and then she shoves down the latch and skitters out round the large oak doors, bringing them shut again with a clumsy *slap*.

I hold my ground for a moment, overwhelmed by the stench of cinnamon that's taken hold of the mansion once more, and then I glance back up at Germo, who's shoved himself into his suit trousers. And nothing else.

I guess that, in itself, might've been enough of a shock for the cleaning lady.

"She say she bring you a something."

"Really?"

He nods back.

"That's *all* she said?"

He gives me one of those stoic grins, and then one of his own Gallic shrugs.

Maybe the first one I've seen him do.

Perhaps because we've suddenly grown a little more familiar over the past few hours.

"She also say that she did not think there was nobody home, and so she decide to clean a little."

"That was very nice of her, what time is it?"

"About midday."

Well, it's not like the cleaning lady came in at the crack of dawn or anything.

But, still, a *Sunday*.

Something about it doesn't seem right.

"She leaves the thing in the kitchen."

"Okay," I say, and then with another, most likely, *lingering* glance over his bare chest, I slink off in the direction of the kitchen.

✳ ✳ ✳

As promised, there is something for me in the kitchen.

And, in here, it absolutely *reeks* of cinnamon, which dries up my mouth despite the impromptu drink of water I had in the en suite.

At least I know that she has been hard at work in here. Good thing too, all things considered. Though I might not have done much in the way of cooking, I certainly know how to make a mess 'not cooking' almost better than anyone.

All the plastic packages I left in the sink, all the emptied, up-turned tins on the side, have been relegated to oblivion, and any trace of dirty crockery, or cutlery, is impossible to find.

She really is thorough.

I wonder if she felt a little annoyed at my ill treatment of the mansion . . . or maybe that's another reason why she so much re-sents guests coming here to visit.

They just make an *awful* mess to be cleaned up.

The *thing* that's waiting for me ends up to be a white plastic bag—what else would fit with the colour scheme?—and I can see that it's a rather odd shape.

Only one way to find out.

I dig into the plastic bag, causing it to rustle, and I feel some-thing cold—*ice* cold—inside. It doesn't take much further in-vestigation to realise that whatever it is that's inside the bag, it's made of glass. A bottle.

I liberate it from the plastic bag and see that it's a bottle of champagne. I look to the golden foil wrapped about the neck, and then to the yellow-tinged—or is that supposed to be gold too?—label stuck onto it.

Also inside, I find a box of chocolates, which I guess accounts for the strange shape of the bag, and why I couldn't guess right away that it was a bottle inside.

Attached to the box of chocolates is a plain white envelope.

It's a miniature size, and just from brushing my fingertips against it, I know that it's that weighty type of paper that costs an absolute fortune.

My name: 'Anna,' is written out in florid, black handwriting.

I tear it off the box of chocolates and then peel it open with a fingernail. There's a note inside, though that's not particularly the surprising part.

I read over the message, all written out in that same, florid, black handwriting:

Dearest Anna,

Hope you're having a 'ball' in the mansion.

Was just trudging about through town and happened to come across these two, and thought they might be appropriate for you and your latest beau.

Relax. Have fun. Come back smiling.

Faithfully yours,

Brian

I have to read the note several times to really appreciate it in its entirety.

First of all, it's the gesture, which, knowing Brian as I do, I realise isn't all that out of character. And, I suppose, neither is this statement about the 'beau' . . . though it does sicken me to the gut about *how* he could have known about me and Germo considering that neither of us has so much as been outside of the mansion since we got here last night.

Then again, if it's as I suspect, that Brian has this place wired for sound, if not video, it's not all that surprising.

But I really don't think that'd be the case. Because, if I know anything at all about Brian, it's that he absolutely *abhors* anything like that . . . well as long as it's equipment like that hanging about *his* premises, if it's another person's property, well, that's just business.

No, he wouldn't have bugged his own place, which leads me into thinking that there can only be one, or maybe two, other explanations.

The first would be that, as I really don't want to imagine, Germo is broadcasting a minute-by-minute report of his activities, and taking pains to be extremely accurate, not to mention sly. Though, it seems a little perverse to me that the report would get to Randolfo, before getting back to Brian himself.

But, even standing there, feeling the warmth of the sunlight drifting in through the kitchen windows, I know that the more likely scenario, and the one that makes me feel much *more* of an idiot, is that Brian knew, all along, just how relations between me and Germo would play out.

Right down to the day.

Because, after all, he was the one who had Germo meet me at the airport in the first place. So why shouldn't Brian have had his own choice in picking out my eye candy?

Why not, indeed?

I guess that just goes to show that you can never fully escape the clutches of Brian Mathewson. Maybe that's just another reason never to even entertain the idea of crossing him.

And all the more reason to take care with this proposal of Randolfo's.

* * *

Back upstairs, I have the luck to catch sight of Germo just as he leaves the shower. He has a fluffy white towel wrapped about his waist. It only reaches a few inches above his knee though, and I guess he couldn't manage to find anything bigger.

He gives me a smile, and then asks me for a favour. If I'd head down to his van, like a good girl, and grab a hold of a sports bag he has in the boot.

But I'm never a good girl unless I can help it.

Especially before I've showered.

So, twenty minutes later, after we've both got ourselves all tired out again, and this time washed ourselves both off once more in the en suite shower, I do head down to the van, all done-up in my dressing gown and smelling of that expensive lemon-scented shower gel. Keys in hand.

I navigate the front hall, sucking in my breath as I stomp over that cinnamon reek which is now going to cling to the mansion like a pox, and out down those wide stony steps to where the turtle-shell green, hunk of a van waits, in all its tinted-window glory.

I brave the dirt driveway, and with a *toot* of the horn, I get the van unlocked, and then bring the back door swinging open. There I find the sports bag.

For a moment I have the urge to have a dig through it. Just to find out what Germo might be packing, if anything at all, and I even cast a look off over my shoulder, as if he might've snuck his way downstairs to check on me . . . just to test my character, to see if I'm as nosey as my reputation suggests.

And it's then that I see a small, hatchback car. A cheery, canary-yellow colour. And the cleaning lady sitting there at the wheel.

At first I think that I can get away with it, that I can look away before she realises me there, but, as if she's got that same tingling sense I have for when people are watching, she twists her head towards me.

I see the tissues clutched in her fist. And the tears running down her cheeks. The caked-on makeup coming down in clumps.

I wait, feeling my heart leaping up to my throat, and my pounding pulse tickling me from the inside. I blink several times as she stares at me, and then I watch her bow her head, and turn the ignition.

The tiny car's engine rumbles to start and, with a crunch of tyres, she pulls out, and heads off along the narrow dirt road. Driving quickly.

Even from where I stand, I can hear the tyres sliding on the dirt, never quite getting their grip fully.

The last part happens in slow motion, though. And that's when I see her veer, inexplicably off to the right.

Off the edge of the path.

Down the steep slope.

CHAPTER EIGHTEEN

A lump sticks in my throat. My blood runs cold, and then hot, then cold again. A tingling sensation breaks out across the surface of my skin, and I feel sick. Rippling nausea rising up in me, and stinging its way upwards, towards my mouth.

All at once I feel a heavy plume of cinnamon hit me. And I taste the bile mixing with it. It takes all my strength to keep myself from vomiting. Even to keep myself standing upright.

It's as if I'm watching the whole thing play out in slow motion.

That canary-yellow car tumble over on its side. Crumpling a little more each time it rolls. The *crunch-crunch* of breaking glass, and the warping of metal.

Soon it slips out of sight.

There's a final and profound *thud* as it hits the bottom.

And I stand there, all the blood rushing up to my face, and feeling the blood running colder and colder through my body.

All I can think about is that the bugs have stopped. That they've ceased their crazed sounds just for a moment, as if they realise the gravity of what I've just witnessed. What I'm *still* witnessing.

And then, all at once, I break out into action.

I don't care about the dirt beneath my feet. Or the rocks that dig into my bare soles.

I just run.

* * *

When I reach the cusp of the dirt path, I look over, and down into the valley.

It's a long way. So far down that the sun shining overhead doesn't have a chance of penetrating the gloom.

I can just about make out the battered shape of the canary-yellow car down there.

I hold my hand up to keep the glare of the sun out of my eyes, and I try to peer into the wreckage, to see if the cleaning lady is moving at all.

But I can't see anything.

I listen to the *tick-tick* of the engine as it runs itself down, and I see one of the back wheels still spinning.

I calculate the grade of the slope. Steep. Too steep for me not to go tumbling after her. And the makeup of the slope is just shingle, and loose rock.

There's nothing I can do for her down there.

I have to get help. That's what I have to do now.

I glance back down, still determined to see any movement at all there, to find some hope that everything, *really*, will be okay.

My mind becomes a flurry with odd thoughts and situations. Of promises that I'll realistically never be able to keep. That, if the cleaning lady can just pull through, *I'll* take the blame for everything. For having made her cry. Having made her drive off so quickly, and so recklessly.

Yes, that's right. It's *all* my fault.

And, with that thought on my mind, I take off running back to the mansion.

* * *

I'm a gibbering wreck when I get to Germo, which is odd considering that I never have the same problem whenever I'm killing someone.

He acts quickly, asks me again for the sports bag, and I fetch it for him.

He paws through the bag and gets dressed in what can only be described as casual clothes: a blue-and-white-striped, polo-neck shirt, cargo shorts, and a pair of beige, leather sandals.

He takes off running though, beating his way along the dirt track. He doesn't glance back once at me, to where I stand on the wide stone steps of the mansion, too much in shock to go any further forwards.

Only when the panic gets too much, and I find myself wanting to cry, do I fold over on myself and sit on the cool, stone step.

I sit there, my knees tugged way up to my chest, and feeling the warming sun on my shoulders.

This should've been such a nice day. A *good* day. I had been planning for us to go down to the beach, to take a visit together to San Floriano. I'm sure Germo would be much happier going skinny dipping in the lapping sea rather than standing upon the promenade in that stuffy black suit of his.

I watch on as he reaches the cusp of the dirt path. And I can see the same thoughts going through his mind, him looking down there into the shadows of that valley, considering whether or not he can make it down.

He glances back along the path, and then, apparently without another thought, he ducks down and slides his way down into the valley.

And out of sight.

* * *

I pass a long while of worrying. I feel the sweat seeping out from my skin. Dampening the dressing gown. That scent of cinnamon is still so strong, seeming to stream its way out of the mansion, and wash over me.

I can taste blood in my mouth. And I realise that I've been working the inside of my cheek with my teeth, causing a gash there. Bringing blood to the surface.

I stop doing it as soon as I realise it and feel the pump of tension in my mouth, the blood all welling up there.

I tell myself lies again. That I'll get up in ten seconds, go over and look into the valley. See if Germo needs any help with his rescue efforts of the cleaning lady.

Those ten seconds go by, of course they do.

And then the next.

And the next.

A *crack* echoes about the landscape.

Something in the car snapping off. Or maybe a component exploding.

That's what, finally, does break me out of my daze, gets me up and heading back along the dirt path.

I hear the *crunch* of the dirt beneath my still-bare feet and think to myself, getting all giddy, that I'll have to take another shower after this. If only for the sake of my feet.

I feel strangely calm as I approach the point where the car slipped off the edge. My pulse slows. I see the tyre tracks in the dirt. The deep ruts where I can see the cleaning lady tried to apply the brakes.

But too late.

I stare off down into the valley. Into the shadows. I feel the sun beating against the back of my neck, and a bead of sweat trickle down my spine, send a ticklish sensation tingling across my nerves.

I can still see the shape down there. The shape of the car in the gloom.

It all seems intact. I can't see any flames, at least. No smoke either.

My breath hitches in my throat. That cinnamon scent seems to linger all around me. And I can taste nothing else in my mouth now, the cinnamon even stronger than the blood.

I can hear the gentle *crunch* and *crumble* of the footfalls down in the valley, but out of sight. I strain my eyes trying to work out whether or not I can see Germo down there, stumbling about the wreckage, perhaps now propping up the cleaning lady, helping her on to safety.

But I can't see anything.

I pull back from the edge, my stomach rebelling on me, my mind playing out just how it might've felt for the cleaning lady to go tumbling over and over in that car.

I scan a little further along. Further along in the shadows of the valley. I wonder what I should do next. If I should locate a phone in Brian's mansion, call up the emergency services.

As long as I can find someone on the other end who can speak English. And call them out here to help.

But first I should check on Germo. See if he's got himself into trouble too. And so I do.

✶ ✶ ✶

My voice echoes back at me off the opposite side of the valley, off the rugged terrain, the rocks and pebbles, and the dirt.

I get no reply.

I call out again.

Same result.

Over to my side, I can hear scrabbling. The sound of pebbles rolling and skittering. The gentle *patter* of rocks being displaced. And a gentle *groan* of someone clambering their way up a steep slope.

On instinct, I swivel about in the direction of the sound. And then I see him, I see Germo there, a good fifty or more paces away from me, helping himself up out of a particularly steep angle of the valley. Bringing himself up out of the shadows and back out into the beaming, midday, sunlight.

My muscles all pull tight, and before I know what I'm doing, I'm running.

Running to him.

Jabbering nothings at him.

As I get closer, he pulls himself back out onto the dirt path. He pants. His previously spotless clothes are now covered in the pale orange dust. He has a large tear in the left knee of his cargo shorts. And I can see blood oozing out from the wound, shining dully in the sunlight.

He looks to me, his face also covered in dust, discolouring his blond hair. And though he looks at me, it's like he's looking right *through* me, out to the other side.

As I reach out for him, he gives a slight snort, and, after a brief pause, lays his arms about me, pulls me to his chest.

I do my best to hold off my question for as long as I can, but, in the end, I know that I'm only suspending the inevitable, that sooner or later I'm going to have to know the answer.

And so I ask.

"Is she . . . ?"

He shakes his head.

And I press my face into his polo shirt, soaked in sweat and dust.

CHAPTER NINETEEN

W e go back into the mansion, and though Germo is obviously also in shock, he seems to be holding it together the best out of the two of us. So he pours out two glasses of water, complete with ice, and a slice of lemon, from the bag of lemons that I recall the cleaning lady bringing us that morning, along with the rest of the groceries, and Brian's gift.

Though I don't feel much like putting anything past my lips, I find a thirst taking me over just as soon as the brim of the glass touches my lips.

I gulp the water down.

Feel that refreshing tang of lemon striking the back of my throat. Bringing me back to my senses. Revitalising me.

Once I've finished the glass, I just breathe in the lemon scent of the glass, the slice of lemon at the bottom. Just losing myself in its zest.

Only when I lay the glass down on the marble kitchen top do I realise just how warm *I* am, how I'm still sweating as if I was still out there in the direct sunlight, rather than inside . . . here in this nice, shady mansion.

All I can hear is the sound of the wind picking out outside. And the slight *pip-pip* of the odd larger grain of dirt making contact with the windows, or one of the steel drainpipes outside.

Germo leans up against the kitchen counter, while I finally have the presence of mind to pull up one of the white-wood barstools and plump myself down on it.

I expect a swirling, nauseous sensation to take hold of me, but instead I go totally calm. My mind seems to have cooled down. And now I can see things a little better.

I can act with a little more pragmatism.

I glance up at Germo, still covered from head to toe in pale orange dust. And the blood still trickling down from his left kneecap. "What should we do now?" I say. "Call the police?"

Germo's own glass of water is still half-finished, and he holds it dangling down at his side, his grip limp as he holds it. He blinks a couple of times, as if trying to get shot of some daze, and then he shakes his head.

I feel the wrinkles break out on my forehead before I realise my confusion. "Why not?" I say. "Isn't that what you're supposed to do when something like this happens?"

Germo remains fixed on some kitchen tile. "No, we cannot."

I wait for a moment, thinking that I'm going to have to nudge him for further explanation, because, frankly, that will just not wash.

But he goes on without my prompting.

"My boss will not *allow* it."

I think about questioning him, but realise that it'll be in vain. Who am I kidding? I know just where Germo's loyalties lie, I know that he looks up only to his employer, and no one else.

But, then again, is it any different between me and Brian?

. . . Brian, yes, this might be a good time to get in touch with Brian, even in danger of incurring his wrath.

It was *his* cleaning lady after all. He was the one who employed her here.

I decide that I can't just let the conversation hang like that, though, and so I add, "And now? What do we do?"

Germo remains serious. His face fixed in a stone-like complexion. "Now? You should leave this just to me. To me and the boss."

I suppose there's really nothing else for me to do, or for me to say, so I just fill up my glass and drink more water.

✷ ✷ ✷

Germo gets me all sat down in the living room, on that expansive white leather sofa, and he heads back upstairs to go and catch a shower. When I ask him, half joking, whether or not he has a fresh pair of clothes, he remains serious, tells me that he has.

I guess that sometimes dry wit just doesn't carry across language barriers.

Only when I get stretched out on the sofa do I realise just how uptight I've been throughout the whole of this terrible thing.

I lie there, still only wrapped in my fluffy dressing gown, and I prop my feet up on the opposite arm of the sofa, staring blankly at the TV.

It flickers away on mute, showing some Spanish soap opera. The screen constantly blinks between well-made-up starlets, to the even-more made-up older ladies of the cast.

And that's without even a mention for the male members of the cast.

But it's enough for me to focus on. Just those overly expressive faces, and the quick cuts between scenes. From one revelation to the next. One plot twist after the next.

What I really like, though, are the establishing shots. The ones of the firm, sandy beaches, and the glittering seas, the swaying palm trees.

I wish *I* could get myself some of that . . . and then I realise that the beach is just around the corner. After all, that was the plan for today.

Maybe something about this horrible day can still be salvaged.

I guess I'll just have to see if I feel up to it.

Once I hear Germo clunking about upstairs, apparently finished with his shower, I manage to wrench myself up off the sofa, and in the direction of the front hall.

As I step over the marble floor, I notice how it's still sopping wet, hasn't dried from where the cleaner has run her mop over it this morning.

And I think about the person who held that mop was alive only a matter of hours ago.

And now she's dead.

As I climb the staircase, make my way back towards the master bedroom, I seem to get absolutely pummelled by that cinnamon stench, and I remind myself to prop open all the windows and doors later, later when I've got my head more together.

When I enter the master bedroom, I find that the air smells of Germo's cologne, along with its unusual cranberry tang. And I breathe it in. Taste it on my tongue. And I feel better about things. More clear headed.

Germo smiles warmly at me as he puts on a fresh pair of cargo shorts, and another polo shirt, this time a salmon-pink colour. He pops the collar and then works at fixing on a golden watch to his wrist. "The boss will be arrive in some minutes."

"Okay," I say, feeling a little sturdier on my feet, less of the tingling passing over my skin.

He puckers his lips, and then glances at the face of the newly fitted watch. Then he looks back at me, those grey eyes of his doing that swirling trick of theirs. That *liquid* thing.

"I go down and help, yes?"

I nod, and manage a half smile.

He shifts his way over to me, and I see that he has washed the pale orange dust off his beige sandals, and that they look just as slick and smooth as if he'd just plucked them out of a shop window.

He leans into me, his heat washing over me, and his stubble rubs against my face as he lays a sweet kiss on my lips.

"Maybe another shower?" he says.

"Yes," I reply, "that might help, I suppose."

He smiles a little more widely, and then he heads on out of the master bedroom, and leaves me alone.

All alone again.

I think a lot about taking the shower, but, instead, remember that I'm supposed to be calling Brian. There're quite a few things for us to speak about, all things considered.

Not least Randolfo's offer to me . . . even though this thing with the cleaning lady seems to have taken precedence all of a sudden.

And so, shirking my fears of those dreaded roaming charges, I flip my mobile on, wait for it to load a network—something cryptically called: 'OceNet'—and I jab my way through the options to the one marked as simply 'Brian.'

I stab the Call button and listen to the gentle, almost catlike purr of the unfamiliar, Spanish dialling tone.

∗ ∗ ∗

"Anna?"

Brian sounds like he's answering the call from the bottom of a well.

A very *echoey* well.

"Hi," I say, my voice wavering all over the place even with that single syllable.

There's a gruff clearing of the throat on the other end, the sound of footsteps, of him no doubt skulking off into some dark place where we won't be heard, and then, "What's wrong?"

His tone is like that of a disgruntled parent. It's as if the roles were reversed, as if Brian was my dad and he was off on holiday, and I was calling to tell him the house had burned down . . . or I'd just had a thousand-strong house party and was now dealing with the fallout.

And that's where Daddy comes in.

I think about where to start. Just where I *should* start. But I come up blank.

The first thing my mind puts in front of me is the thing with Randolfo, so that's what I blurt out next, asking Brian's opinion of him.

Brian goes all quiet on the other end of the line for a while, and I wonder if this, no doubt extortionate, roaming network has lost our connection.

I decide to check. "So," I say, "what do you think of him? What do you know about him? Like I said, he says the two of you are partners. Something like that."

The pause on Brian's end extends even further.

"Hello?" I say, now almost certain we've been cut off.

"I . . . uh, well, yes, I *suppose* you could put it that way, 'partners,' I mean."

This is already growing to be too much for my over-bombarded brain to take. "Can you just be straight with me," I say, "just for once, I mean. I *am* on holiday after all."

"Straight with you?" Brian says, sounding infinitely perplexed.

"Yes, you know, it's the thing where you just say exactly what's going on, no beating about the bush, just straight *truth*."

"Yes, fine," he says, and then, apparently regaining some of his trademark bravado, "I think I've come across this *truth* thing once in a while."

"Then what's your dealing with this Randolfo Perez, what's your connection with him?"

"Oh, nothing special, just straight publicity work, everything above board. Really, no skeletons in the cupboards at all."

I lower my voice, decide to be a little more direct. "And what about the guy you had meet me at the airport, the *Germo* guy. What's your connection with him?"

"Oh, he's a good man, know him personally."

"He works for Randolfo."

"Yes, that's right. But we also have a good working relationship. He really can be depended on out there . . . not with anything *really* serious, though, of course, bombing back and forth from the airport, showing my favoured ladies a good time, those sort of things. Wouldn't trust him with scissors, if that's what you mean. But good for all the dopey stuff."

"Is that what you tell *all* your 'favoured' ladies?"

I hear the smile enter his voice. "Oh no, my dear, but your intellect is something to cherish, it really is, I'm sure you will have figured this one out right away. That little present of mine, the champagne and the chocolates, really a joke, old girl. Just my way of showing that you're the one that's won, that you'd never fall so hook, line and sinker for such a blatant move as that one. Putting that hunk of a man in your way."

I stay quiet for that one. There's some well-worn phrase about not letting on you're a dope by not opening your mouth . . . but I reckon there's scope for a similar one along the lines of *certainly* not seeing your way to correcting someone when they *over*estimate you.

All par for the course with mine and Brian's power games between one another.

He thinks I'm bright.

I *know* I'm not as bright as he thinks I am.

And that's where it ends till he finds out different . . .

I decide that now would be prudent to change the subject, so I do.

"And what do you think about this offer of his? I mean, he wants me to take on his daughter, and 'teach her everything I know,' as he put it. What's the thinking behind that?"

"Oh, I would think it's as straight as it sounds." He hesitates, grumbles something under his breath that I'm not supposed to hear—an extremely annoying habit of Brian's. "You must understand that Perez is a wealthy man, that he owns a good chunk of the country out there."

"All very much above board, of course?"

Again, I hear the smile in Brian's voice. "How else?" His tone straightens out. "And with such great amounts of money—and *power*—I think he finds himself somewhat exposed to the more, ah, *unsavoury* aspects of life out there."

"If he's worried about someone making off with his daughter then why doesn't he just employ a bodyguard twenty-four hours a day, you know, like he's got Germo looking out for me?"

"A good question, and one that I cannot answer. Why don't you ask *him?*"

I think about telling Brian straight out that I don't trust Randolfo, not for one second, but I hold off since I don't know the full details of his relationship with Brian.

"Anyway, what's it to do with me?" Brian says. "I mean, are you really calling me up to ask *permission* to work with Randolfo?"

I keep quiet, because I know that's exactly the reason I called Brian . . . or one of the reasons. Me and Brian have always had a somewhat handshake-based relationship, and I know that I wouldn't want to go behind his back. Now I decide would be a good time to change the subject. And so I tell him about the cleaning lady.

There's another long silence on the other end as Brian absorbs this titbit, and then says, "I'm terribly sorry to hear that."

When I answer him, my throat is dry and my voice feels all feeble. "What was her name?"

Brian pauses a moment, but I don't think it's to search his mind. He might be flippant with other things, but never with employees, people who do him a good job. He *never* forgets names. "Señora Esmeralda," he says, finally.

I sense that the line between us has grown heavy, as if this piece of news really has soured Brian's previously good mood. And I think of hanging up there and then, before deciding to push the boat out, to ask him the question that bugs me.

"Germo . . . he says that he doesn't want to bring the police in, doesn't want them to come and investigate. What do you think about that?"

Brian sounds far away when he answers and, in a way, I guess he is. "I would cross Randolfo at my peril," he says, before adding, "Do take care out there, Anna, won't you? And, just like I said on the note: come back smiling."

He hangs up on me, just like that.

I think back over his words. Over what he's just said. About me having to take care.

I flush it about my mind, try to see it from every angle. But there's no other explanation. How *can* there be any other explanation?

Brian *always* says just what he means . . . when he's speaking frankly, that is.

As I hang up the call, see that it's taken the best part of fifteen minutes, the stomach of the thrifty me inside does a little flip. Sinks a little into nausea. But then I remember that I'm halfway to being a millionaire . . . and if I take Randolfo's money I'll be *all* the way there, and on my way to a new life.

To a *different* life.

A life away from all this killing.

And wouldn't that be nice?

Just one last thing for me to do.

With a final sigh, I turn my mobile off, watch its crystalline display sink into the battery-dead black, and then replace it in my bedside drawer.

As I lie my mobile in there, I notice the grip of *Solecito*.

Just like always, I keep it tucked away in the drawer while I sleep at night, so that it's ready for me to yank out at a moment's notice.

Something within me, maybe it's the tension, or the emotional turmoil wreaking its way through my chest, forces me to wiggle my hand in there and take hold of it.

I look it over.

Try to see if there's anything wrong.

Something *feels* wrong.

The weight?

No, the same.

Loaded?

I flush the magazine. Weigh that.

Yes, that's . . . and then I see what the trouble is.

My eyes linger down over the bullets all snug within the magazine, and I count them all. See that there are *two* missing.

My mind bends, weaves in and out.

I count my shots.

Well, there's only been *one* so far. The one I fired off into the ceiling. But, as for the other one, when did it . . . and then it strikes me.

Germo.

Germo's shot *Solecito*.

But when?

Outside, I hear the churning of an engine. The crunch of dirt beneath heavy-duty wheels, and I flinch slightly at the sound. Check myself over. Realise that I'm meant to be taking a shower.

And so I slip *Solecito* back into the drawer and make for the en suite, bringing the door shut with a *slam* behind me.

CHAPTER TWENTY

Though I'm aware of the falling warm water, the feel of it as it slicks up my skin, and dampens my hair for the second time that day, I'm not experiencing it.

My mind is simply getting away from me. Snicking and catching like rusted-up machinery. This was *supposed* to be an escape. Now what is it? What have I managed to get myself in the middle of? And, the question that boggles my mind more than anything: just who is this Germo guy I spent the night with?

Who's still here now.

And, for all I know, consorting with a bunch of other goons.

The answer frightens me . . . because I don't know.

I only stand the water for about five minutes before it becomes too hot to bear, what with the stifling humidity that seems to penetrate every nook and cranny of the mansion today.

I get out of the shower sweating. But at least it's *clean* sweat. And I seem to have got myself shot of most of the pale orange dirt. Managed to purge it from my skin.

But I can still feel the dirt inside my mouth. Can still taste the blood on my tongue. And I feel a shudder clasp hold of my bones and shake me inside out.

My teeth chatter. Great big, enamel-crunching chatters.

I wish myself away from this place.

Can I still get away from this place?

Escape all this craziness?

I'm a big girl and, what's more, I'm a big girl with a *gun*.

Who's to say that I can't extricate myself from this place somehow?

I flip down the lid of the white-wooden toilet seat with a *thunk*, and then sit down on top of it. I stare at the white-tiled wall, and then to the drops on the inside of the glass shower cubicle as they grow and merge and stream down the glass.

Have I been sleepwalking my way through this holiday?

What other explanation is there for the mess I find myself in now?

I grab another few seconds of staring before I snap into action.

Now it's time for me to get shot of all this . . . of this . . . this *sham* of a holiday.

I launch myself back onto my feet and sweep into the master bedroom. I slide my suitcase out from beneath the bed, and set about hurriedly packing it. Simply chucking in everything I can find within reach. No logic to it.

Once I'm finished, I dress quickly in a pair of jeans and one of my old t-shirts: the ones I keep specifically for travelling, or sleeping, and then I snap my little, bulky silver-grey, hard-case luggage up onto its plastic wheels, and shove it halfway across the room.

It skitters over the marble floor and, by some minor miracle, doesn't flop over in a heap.

I dip into the bedside table drawer and pluck out *Solecito*.

All ready to go now.

Just *try* and let them stop me.

I stab my pair of battered, travelling trainers onto my feet, draw the retractable handle of the suitcase out with a *snap*, and then, holding *Solecito* down by my side, I make for the door to the master bedroom.

* * *

The mansion is so quiet. But the cinnamon smell still dominates everything. That smell, though, has gone beyond being annoying, and now it just makes me sad. I know that, once it has faded away, no one will ever smell it again.

Unless the next cleaning lady Brian employs just happens to use the same brand of floor cleaner.

The plastic wheels of my luggage skitter along the well-washed marble floor, and I make for the stairs which lead down to the garage. Already knowing just what I have to do.

I slide the keys off the hook I left them on and then give the fob a squeeze.

A *toot* of the horn, and a flash of the amber lights, and Box Wagon is all open.

Ready for business.

I slide into the driver's seat, dragging my luggage up into the passenger's floor space, then I stick the keys into the ignition with a grating *scrape*. Switch on. Listen to the *hum* and *purr* of the engine. Feel the vibrations dancing through my fingertips. Passing right through to my bones.

My palms are sweaty as I disengage the handbrake, but I keep enough of a hold to stay in control. And I plant it downwards, with yet another, bad-sounding, mechanical *scrape*.

As I inch forwards, I hear the mechanism of the garage doors whirring into action. And I watch them slowly fold back. The daylight dribble into the garage. Through onto the cement floor. And then I wait.

My heart pounds harder. My giddy thoughts come and go. Too slippery to hang onto anything for long.

The only thought that stays with me is the urge to drive. And to drive *fast*.

As the garage doors leave just enough space for me to inch Box Wagon beneath, I pull forwards, no longer caring if there is quite enough room to clear the base of the doors.

As I stick the accelerator to the floor and grind my way up the steep incline of the garage drive, I hear the mournful grating as the base of the garage doors strips the paintwork from the roof of Box Wagon.

In my panic, I promise myself that I'll pay Brian the cost of the damages, in the unlikely event that he won't decide to just stick it straight on his insurance.

And I plough upwards. Feeling the force of the car all around. My fingers clasping the wheel tighter as I move up and out, *escaping* the mansion.

Dirt and stones crunch beneath the mighty weight of Box Wagon, and I eye the dirt road up ahead. But there's a problem. A reason I don't simply gun the throttle and beeline for the airport.

Three cars. All of them like Germo's: vans. Tinted windows. Exhaust pumping out in plumes. They all box me into the garage. Don't allow me to pass.

I realise that one of them *is* Germo's van.

As I glare out at them from beneath my windscreen, I consider pressing my luck, trying to shove my way through with brute force.

But I know that Box Wagon, though it might be a brute, this time will simply be unable to get through.

It's been outgunned.

I think back to the motorbike. Wonder if that might've been my best bet after all.

Maybe in another life.

I look about them, along those anonymous tinted windows before I finally pick out Germo. He stands there, a semi-automatic rifle in his hands. Staring down the barrel.

Pointing right at me.

CHAPTER TWENTY-ONE

Everything goes impossibly silent. The engines all ebb out of my hearing. My vision blurs. And I feel myself shaking all over.

But there's nothing I can do.

Nothing at all.

Not now.

They have me with my back up against the wall.

I hear Germo shout out. His shout is loud enough to be heard through the thick glass of the Box Wagon. "Hands on head!"

I look to *Solecito*, nestled in my lap, and I think about making a go of it.

I know that, all things being equal, I'd have a good chance of being able to take Germo down with a headshot.

But, though things may be many things in this situation, one thing they certainly are not is equal.

I have no choice.

Not if I want to live.

My heart feels like a stone. Sinking down in my chest. My blood runs cold and my palms are clammy. And a voice keeps telling me over and over again to do just what Germo says. Because, if I don't, that'll be the end.

As my mind gets away from me, I slip back to a time with Ben and Josie. All of us visiting a zoo. Going to see the animals. A time after me and Arnold decided to go our separate ways . . . after *I* decided it was better if we went our separate ways.

We have a bag of nuts with us. Something about wanting to feed the monkeys . . . but the zoo keepers said no, and so we're chomping our way through them ourselves. And I can't help but think just how they taste like munching on earth, but there're so moreish at the same time. So much so that I can't resist another fistful.

We're all walking through this forest or, at least, in my mind it's a forest. Maybe it's just greenery, just some trees surrounding us on all sides. And I can hear the birds twittering. Can smell animal dung seemingly all around.

Ben and Josie.

Both of them holding my hands.

One at either side.

Both of them smiling.

All three of us munching on the monkey nuts.

I snap back. I recognise the deeply engrained lines on Germo's face. Know that if I don't do what he asks that I'll be dead. Gone.

Forever.

But I still have something to live for. I have to live for my kids. Because, though I might be a lousy mother . . . a *terrible* mother, I still *am* their mother.

They *need* me, even if they don't know it yet.

And, what's more, when I get out of this, I'm determined to show them how true that is.

I lift my hands up so that Germo can see them. I lay them down on the top of my head. My heart thumps hard in my throat. In my ears. And right to the base of my tongue.

Germo is approaching Box Wagon now. Tentative. Eyes unflinching. Mouth fixed in a tight pout. The semi-automatic rifle pointed right at me. And, I'm sure, pointed right between my eyes.

How I'd love for us to have a duel. For us to be on equal terms. A duel with pistols. None of this heavy-handed rifle bullshit.

I notice that the drivers of the other cars, those other vans identical to Germo's—what with them all being that same turtle-shell green colour—have all got out.

Tinted-green sunglasses, to match their vans.

Hard expressions.

Bustling muscles.

They all have their own rifles in their hands now. And they're leaning on the bonnets of their vans, pointing them at me too.

There really is no way out now.

No point wishing that I'd taken the motorbike instead.

Even though it's a long time since I last rode a motorbike, what with it being back in my moody, introspective teenage years, I'm sure that I could do it again.

If I *really* had to.

Doesn't look like Germo and his boys are going to give me a chance, though.

Poor, little me.

* * *

They slip a pair of white cable ties about my wrists and tighten them so hard that my hands turn white, or maybe even a light green, from the pressure.

I guess they're taking no chances.

No chances at all.

One thing I notice, the same time they're cuffing me, is one of the other men come stalking along and, wearing white gloves, extricate *Solecito* from my lap.

As he turns round and stalks back off in the direction of his car, he holds the pistol away from him as if it was a dirty nappy.

Next, Germo eases me up from the driver's seat, and over the step and back down onto the dirt path. He is firm but gentle with me.

A little like he was last night.

And he helps me across the dirt track and over to his own van. The van that he's shepherded me along in during this entire trip, it seems.

With his support, I get up into the back of the van. This time going in through the sliding door, and having to take up my place in the back seats. Only as I reluctantly sink into one of the over-squidgy, ink-black leather seats do I realise that Germo has put up a kind of mesh between myself and the front seats.

The kind of chicken wire-type mesh they use on dog kennels.

Is that what I am now? A dangerous animal.

Though I know the situation is grave, and deeply serious, I can't help wondering if Germo's taking this precaution because of my appetite last night . . . what is it they say about if you don't have your humour, why, then you don't have anything at all?

But there's nothing I can do except go crazy, show them a bit of fang and make some noise . . . so I simply sit back quietly and look forward to the ride.

CHAPTER TWENTY-TWO

watch the mansion recede into the distance, that great big, *white* monstrosity slipping beneath the horizon. As we go along on the dirt track, I do my best to get a look down the slope, into those shadows where the cleaning lady ended up. But Germo is driving too fast for me to see properly.

One thing I *do* know, though, is that she has a bullet hole between the eyes . . . or wherever Germo chose to put it.

What I don't know is *why*.

Only when we emerge out onto the asphalt main road, and take that turn left, do I give up all hope that we might be headed for San Floriano.

Guess we're not going to the beach at all, then.

And we make our way, really *steaming* off along the road. The tyres sounding slick and pounding against the surface.

After about a mile or so, I notice one of the vans sweep out of the file and overtake us, take up the front position. So now there's a van in front, and one behind, like a prison procession or something.

One thing's for certain, though. I *am* a prisoner.

The only thing I'm grateful for, being held like this, is that Germo has seen his way to turning on the air conditioning in the back of the van. So I have an ice-cold stream of air constantly blowing in my face. Stopping me from cooking up like a stuck pig.

We drive on for a long time, it must be at least two hours, before we pull off the main road, the road that leads to the sea, and we head down a narrower route.

I watch other cars drifting by us on the other side of the street. Listen to their engines drone by. And I can't help wishing I was like them. That I was free.

Who knows, if I take my chances, I might be free again.

And soon.

✳ ✳ ✳

We drive for even longer, seeming to take a lot of corners, to turn off onto roads before doubling back on ourselves.

Maybe Germo thinks that I'm somehow following where we're going, making a mental note of the route for some masterstroke later on.

Like I said before, it's always much better when your enemy overestimates you.

That gives you the psychological advantage.

Among other things.

I notice the terrain around us getting lumpier, the boulders cropping up on either side of us, and then those boulders, and the flat dirt plains, giving way to foothills. The brink of some mountain range or other . . . though I guess, for me, coming from the UK, and the biggest landmass there being three thousand foot, that pretty much anything qualifies as a mountain in my eyes.

The roads get windier, and narrower, though I'm glad to see that there are several well-maintained, steel barriers that wrap their way around the corners. And it's good to see that they are well dented, too, suggesting that most of the traffic that's come into contact with them has bounced right back onto the road.

Or bounced right over the edge.

Now that we're rising higher, I feel like the air conditioner is beginning to get up my nose, to turn the back of the van into a kind of freezer or, at the very least, a fridge.

I clutch my arms over my chest, trying to keep warm, and I suck on my tongue, hoping that the neutral taste of my saliva will somehow quiet the rest of my body.

The new-car odour is overpowering back here, and I wonder if Germo snuck out in the middle of the night to clean up in preparation for kidnapping me.

I guess he wanted to make a good impression.

The engine grunts longer and harder as it eats up the hills, taking the switchbacks at high speed. If it wasn't for Germo's skill I would be absolutely terrified . . . scratch that, I *am* absolutely terrified, and I hope for both our sakes that he's concentrating hard in addition to possessing great driving skill.

We rumble along for a while before I watch the brake lights of the van ahead of us shine bright. It's only then that I realise how dark it's got. That we're surely right on the brink of twilight now.

I guess that I zoned out for a long while in the back of the van. My brain and imagination just running wild for a long time. Or maybe I even slept, though I don't remember slipping off or having dreams of any kind.

But maybe it's better to sleep without dreams.

Or nightmares.

The van ahead of us pulls up to a complete stop, and I see up ahead a pair of enormous great black steel gates. There're the kind of gates with poles that rise a good ten feet and have points sharpened at the top.

Though I get the impression that these gates, and the surrounding pointy fences, aren't the limits to this place's security.

The van ahead of us waits. Its exhaust coming out in plumes. Floating up in the air.

On the horizon, just beyond our caravan, I can see the sun setting on the horizon, sending everything into a pinkish shimmer.

Fatalistically, I wonder if this might be the last time that I'll see the sun.

But I don't get much time to think on that one because, before I know it, the black steel gates are opening inwards, and the van ahead is driving inside.

We follow along on its tail.

✶ ✶ ✶

Bright-white floodlights illuminate the place ahead of us. Something that I can only describe as a . . . well, a *castle*.

It has a blocky, vaguely Spanish style to it and it looms over everything. I wonder if it has been painted or if its natural colour is really as I see it.

Sable. Pure, deep, unblemished *black*.

It reminds me of a dark-bottomed cloud lingering on the edge of an otherwise sunny day, that's how it seems out here, nestled in the mountains. Though, I imagine, soon it will come into its own when the night descends and it slips into obscurity.

I guess that the patron of the place must relish *that* prospect.

There are swooping lawns about the grounds too, and a tree-lined avenue which leads up to the main entrance: a road which circles a lightly spraying fountain with a cherub on top, bow playfully held in his fingers.

We round the stone-sculptured cherub, and go past the main entrance.

Perhaps I should be offended that I'm being taken in through the back . . . but, I guess, all things considered, I should probably be grateful that I don't have a bullet in *my* brain.

Not yet, anyway.

Our motorcade proceeds around the castle, and I get the chance to fully take its mass—its sheer *scale*—in properly.

It must be at least five storeys high, and it seems to just stretch on and on forever, at least from this perspective, at ground level.

I notice that most of the rooms have the yellow glow of light too, and wonder whether that's simple arrogance of the owner or if there are really this many people occupying the castle.

We end up arriving in a more modern section of the castle, an area that I can tell, from the youngish people hovering about in chef hats and stained white aprons, must be the kitchen entrance. But this isn't where the vans park up.

Nope.

The motorcade continues on around the endless wall of the castle, and right up to a glowing red light, that stares out menacingly at us.

The driver of the van in front does *something*, scans a card . . . a fingerprint, I don't know . . . and a barrier rises up. The van rumbles on down a slope, and we follow on their tail.

✶ ✶ ✶

When we reach bottom, a fluorescent light blinks on, lighting the place up. And it turns out that we've emerged in a ceiling-to-floor, cement underground car park.

There are several other cars parked and, again, even with me not being the biggest expert of cars, and not wanting to be, I know that all these cars spread out are all top-of-the-range, glistening sports models.

And, most likely, prohibitively expensive.

Surely even beyond my, fairly, upwardly mobile budget.

I feel like someone, somewhere, is draining my bank account just from me looking at them.

The vans, keeping that strict formation they've held all the way to the castle, all swing into their respective spots, all of which are marked out with yellow lines.

All the lines are immaculately painted on.

I look to Germo, who switches off and pulls the keys from the ignition. Then he glances back at me, over his shoulder, for the first time in the whole journey, and then says, "We have arrive Mrs Harris."

If there wasn't a chicken wire mesh between us, he would get a good, old-fashioned clip round the ear. But, as there is, he lives to fight another day.

I watch as the men from the other two vans, the two other drivers, each step down. They're already holding their rifles before they dare set foot on the ground. And I see that, Germo too, has a rifle of his own.

As he rounds the van, he hoists the rifle strap over his shoulder, and then, with a flick of the wrist, snaps open the lock and slides the door open.

I get caught with a rush of warm air. I guess this underground car park gets good and baked during the day. And it smells of warmed-up cement too . . . never a great smell.

As Germo 'helps' me down from the van, I realise how arid the air is down here, and how thirsty I've got over the course of the journey.

I could lick the perspiration off the car windows.

Seriously.

And, confusingly, I also have the urge to go to the toilet. It feels like my bladder is near enough burning a hole through my stomach . . . if that's even *possible*.

But there's not going to be time for any comfort breaks.

Not yet, anyway.

With two of the men flanking, just a couple of steps off the pace, and with Germo tugging me forwards, keeping a strong hold on the cable ties about my wrists, I get a glance in about the garage. Try to see if there's *anything* worth memorising down here.

Just a bunch of sports cars really. Nothing much else to write home about.

And it seems like the patron of the castle, rather like Brian, has a preference for motorbikes too.

There are half a dozen all lined up, all of them gleaming, and in general looking extremely serviceable indeed.

Now, if only I could get shot of these cable ties.

. . . Oh yeah, and these guards with rifles.

Still, that's a piece of knowledge to stow away for a rainy day.

There's a large service lift which one of the men pushes the button to. The metal-grey, probably plastic, button glows orange about the edge, and I listen to a heavy-duty mechanism grind and heave the lift down to us.

I guess it's just as well oiled as everything else down here.

We rise up together, none of us speaking. Just like I've always maintained, good goons should be seen and not heard . . . really just an extension on my Male Theory, but there goes . . . and when we reach our chosen floor there's an almost comedy *ping* sound.

And for some reason I want to shoot one of the men a smile.

Or maybe just shoot them.

We emerge out into a lobby . . . and I begin to think that, maybe, this place is actually a hotel. Or a very posh block of apartments. I look to a woman who's running the reception. She wears a burgundy uniform with a pillar-box hat, and she has on white gloves.

She doesn't so much as look up at us, as the men stomp through her reception area with the rifles they're packing.

Not to mention the prisoner walking among them.

Only when I get a look out a window up here do I realise that we must be near the top floor. From here I can see out onto the surrounding landscape. Beyond the rolling hills, just about shrouded in darkness now, and down onto the road where I can see headlights bobbing along. *Free* people. Going about their *free* lives.

We head onwards, and I get the time to note the floor: ebony-washed marble, and up the walls too. If it wasn't for the high-energy light bulbs that illuminate, I'm sure that this whole place would be smothered in darkness by now.

I reckon the décor would swallow up moonlight in a second.

Another security door greets us ahead and it allows us right on through once one of the goons has smudged his fingertip against the scanner.

That brings us into another, unmanned, reception area. Just a desk standing there. And, up ahead, a pair of pine doors.

To be frank, it's a surprise that they're not black like everything else. But I guess even the most demanding of designers have to make compromises at certain points.

One of the men knocks a couple of times, there's a pause, and then the door opens wide.

And it's Randolfo standing there, looking out.

Of course it is.

CHAPTER TWENTY-THREE

That scent of elderberries washes over me. Seems to make everything, from my nostril hair down, tingle. Makes the blood froth in my veins. And my heart lurch up to my throat. I want to spit. To get that taste out. But I can't. That would be unladylike.

Really. This is the last man on *Earth* I want to see at this point.

But what did I expect?

I take in that lush brown hair of his as it billows down to his neck. I guess that in the space of the previous twenty-four hours he's had it dyed because I can't see any trace of the previous sashes of grey.

Maybe he's had it dyed *specially* for me.

And those rosy brown eyes, they're the next thing that fastens onto me. And once they're fastened on . . . well, they're just like leaches. They simply won't let me go.

And the worst part of it is that *I* can't look away either.

"Anna," he says with a wry smile, "lovely to see you here."

I look beyond him, to what I suppose to be his apartment.

I can see a plush, black moleskin sofa, and a mahogany-coloured coffee table. A little way beyond that, and attached to the wall, a plasma TV.

Not as big as Brian's.

The carpet beneath Randolfo's feet is thick, black and curly, like the hair of a well-kept dog . . . which is to say, certainly unlike any dog *I* might have, or *cat* for that matter, just ask Lizzie.

He smirks at me. "Please, be my guest. Come in," he says, giving the men around me a curt nod, and then beckoning me forward.

If Randolfo stinks of elderberries, then I think, in his apartment, I might well have discovered the source of it all. I half expect to see a tree . . . or do elderberries grow on bushes? . . . sprouting right up out of the black carpet. Big and squidgy and ready to drop right off. If there were any lying about on the floor I would gladly squash them in with my heel. Just try to ruin a bit of Randolfo's home.

That'd boost my spirits.

But, of course, there *are* no elderberries. Of course there aren't, Anna. It's all just my overactive imagination. Me getting all carried away again.

He offers me a place on the black moleskin sofa, and I take him up on it.

He sits too.

I glance down at my wrists that still have the cable ties burrowing into my flesh, and then look to him, hoping that he might get the hint.

He clicks at one of the men, and I see, as he comes round with a quite large, and quite sharp, knife, that it's Germo.

Germo slides the knife against the plastic, makes a rut, and then swipes upwards a little too violently for my liking.

Too violently for someone like me who knows that he bats no eyelid at murdering little old ladies.

But at least now I'm hands-free.

I give both my wrists a little massage, rubbing out that fire-hot glow of pain that the plastic ties have inflicted on me, and then I look back to Randolfo.

And, what do you know, he's smiling.

"I am very sorry that it has come to this, Anna, but I must admit that it is more a matter of security. That you simply *must* accept my proposal, a refusal is out of the question."

I resist the temptation to tell him that what he's doing is an awful lot like blackmail. But bite it back. Just.

"You see, with me, the situation has changed, and it means that it is now necessary for you to accept my proposal right away."

"What's changed?" I say, on instinct, a little annoyed at myself for having given up my silence so willingly.

He layers on his smile a little more. "They are things that you should not concern yourself with. Please, you will just be my guest for a few days, and then I shall let you go."

"So this is your home?"

"Of course," he says, his smile widening even further . . . if at all possible. "I *own* this entire castle, the *Castillo de los Llanos*."

"And you really need that much room for guests?"

He chuckles. "Well, yes, though I believe the correct term would be 'tenants.'"

"So it's just a big apartment complex?"

"Yes, in a certain way," he says. "I suppose you *could* call it like that."

I can feel my heart pounding now, and my blood warming up. And I know that, pretty soon, if I don't watch myself, I'm going to snap.

At least a little.

"So," he says, "the proposal shall go ahead as planned. Beginning from tomorrow"—he tilts his head forwards and fixes me with the bottoms of his eyes—"*Monday*, you shall instruct my daughter, Viviana, on all the necessary skills of your, uh, *trade*."

Not really in any position to bargain, I simply nod my head.

He becomes straight faced. "Now, Anna, you must understand that you need to teach her well, and that when you have finished with her training that she is *at least* bordering on your own competence. Is that clear?"

"How long?"

"One month," he says. "No more."

I think this over, for some reason my mind is switching back to pragmatic mode. Though every other instinct within me is telling me to fight, to struggle as much as I can . . . to *spit* in his eye, if I get the chance . . . the logical part is telling me to stay calm, not to struggle. Because when I *do* let loose, there'll only be one chance to do it right. And after that, well, after that just doesn't bear thinking about.

"Is it possible?" he says, with a pout.

I bite my tongue. *Hard* this time. And I manage a nod. Then a very slight, "Yes."

"Good," he says, spreading on that familiar smarmy smile of his as he rises up off the sofa. "Then everything is arranged, you shall instruct Viviana beginning tomorrow."

"Okay."

He shuffles his way across the carpet, heading for another doorway.

And it's right then that I *know* I have to step in, that I *have* to say something. Otherwise I'm going to regret it forever. "The old lady," I say. "What was that about?"

He stops, turns, and meets my eye.

Those rosy brown eyes of his smoulder away, more like hot coals than embers today, and then he says, "That was necessary," he says, "a necessary evil for me to ensure that I would be allowed to contract you."

"What, why? I don't understand."

"Don't you, Anna?" he says, then gives me the most revolting wink I've ever had the misfortune of being on the receiving end of before slipping through the doorway, and away from the sitting room.

* * *

Soon after . . . well, try five seconds after Randolfo has disappeared, the three men—including Germo—all put their nasty faces back on and they set me back on my feet. March me to the door of Randolfo's apartment.

Well, at least they didn't see their way to placing a fresh set of cable ties over my wrists.

I half expect them to lead me back to the lift, that they'll have some nice, cool, cinderblock place all picked out for me somewhere in the neighbourhood of the underground car park. But, no, they lead me along the black marbled floor to a door about five or six down from Randolfo's apartment.

Just before one of the men does that trick with the fingertip scanner again, I get that prickling feeling all over again, that feeling that I'm being watched.

When I glance back, I see a familiar head poking its head out from one of the doors. Looking out into the corridor.

That *black* hair, and the blond streaks.

And those same rosy brown eyes of her father's.

Viviana.

Just before one of the men shoves me in the back, I get a chance to read her expression. To see the fullness of her lips, the slightly widened eyes.

But it's only once I'm inside the room. Inside what's to be, well, let's face it, my glorified *jail* cell, that I realise that the look on her face was one of concern.

Concern for me.

* * *

The door slams shut behind me and I hear the lock mechanism whirr shut. A pair of bleeps. I look back to see that it's a pine door, just like the one that led into Randolfo's apartment. I guess that the Perez family, having the entire run of this castle, get an apartment each, so Viviana was glancing out from her own place.

Makes me wish that I'd had the good fortune to be a rich man's daughter.

Might not find myself in the fix I'm in right now.

But, nope . . .

The walls are painted a light mauve colour, and the furniture is all pine, I guess to match the door. A slight smell of elderberries clings to this place too, but I guess that's going to be inevitable just about anywhere in Randolfo's castle.

I see a doorway too, and when I investigate I see that it leads to a kitchenette and then, a little beyond that, to a small bathroom . . . well, I say small, but it's most likely about three times the size of the one I have back home.

I guess I've got a little too accustomed to Brian's mansion.

There's a large, steel bath, and a glass shower cubicle with matching steel fixings. And I see that the toilet has a pine seat. That's always novel: matching comfort *and* design.

He has towels too, all spread out for me, on the radiator rails, so that I won't have to suffer drying myself with a cold piece of material in the morning.

Thoughtful.

Once I've concluded my search of the bathroom, I move onto the kitchen. First thing I check is for any sign of knives in the drawers. All of them are blunted, though it's arguable just what damage I might've been able to get away with considering that all the men in this castle seem to carry semi-automatic rifles like other men carry mobiles.

Back in the bedroom, I look to the neatly made bed, and to the small plasma TV that hangs up from the wall over the bed, so I can watch a bedtime story if I like . . . and if I can find an English channel then there might be some hope that I actually might understand it.

Then, remembering just how parched, and how badly I needed that 'comfort break' earlier on, I dash to the toilet, finish up there, and then pour myself out three glasses of water in a row.

Strangely, the water has a slight taste of mint to it. And it's so cold that I wonder if Randolfo has bought up some natural spring beneath the castle, and has the water directly piped up from there, into his tenants' taps.

Feeling thoroughly worn out, just about every single muscle and bone in my body screaming out in pain, I throw myself down on the bedspread.

Moleskin, just like the sofa in Randolfo's apartment.

Guess that he's living proof of 'if it's good enough for me, then it's good enough for you.'

Not that I'm complaining.

Though this is a prison cell, I'm pleasantly taken in by it, I have to admit. Sure, it's nothing more than a studio apartment, but it's cosy, I suppose, in its own way.

I'm first to admit that I've had a long day and so I hope that's my excuse for not putting the pieces of the puzzle together sooner, back in Randolfo's apartment: the business with the cleaning lady, with Señora Esmeralda. Now, though, with a little time, and my heart rate for the first time approaching anything close to normal, I take a moment.

It's so obvious.

I know just what they've done.

And it makes me feel a real fool to have just stood about, on the periphery, and let them do it.

What Germo has done, by shooting Señora Esmeralda with my own gun . . . or, at least, a gun absolutely plastered in my fingerprints, among DNA, no doubt . . . is allow me to be implicated whenever they wish.

So, even if I did escape the castle, I'm certain that the first thing that Randolfo would do would be to get into contact with his people in the police.

And if what Brian said about him not being one to be messed with is right then I'm certain that Randolfo *must* have some pretty good friends in the police.

In the midst of my prospective escape, the police would stop me at the airport. If not before. And I'd find myself being whisked through the Spanish legal system here.

Perhaps if this was England, I wouldn't be as worried as I am now, but the truth is that I've never heard Brian sound as trumped as he did on the phone.

In fact, thinking about it now, he sounded almost scared.

Scared of Randolfo.

I'm sure that, right now, or maybe before, Germo and his two stooges have worked away at *Solecito*, getting it nice and clean so that only my own fingerprints are on it.

What Randolfo has on me is far better than that locking mechanism on the door, or the men with their semi-automatic rifles.

He has me sewn up, and with total legality.

Maybe I should feel furious with myself, ready to punch the wall or something, but the truth is that I feel immeasurably calm. Zen-like, almost. Because I know that there's simply nothing I can do.

I just have to wait this thing out, stay calm, not let on that I'm plotting anything at all, and then trust in Randolfo that he'll let me go when he's got just what he needs from me.

Once he's satisfied I've done my best to train up his daughter to a certain standard.

And if there's one thing I absolutely *abhor* it's having to trust someone else.

But what else can I do?

CHAPTER TWENTY-FOUR

I **guess that I must sleep** because, next thing I know, I can feel the warm glow of the sun beaming in through the window. Its rays splashing all over my face.

I'm still lying on top of the bedspread, on top of that moleskin fabric, and all my body feels stiff, as if I've kept all my muscles constantly flexed throughout the night. The worst of it is with my wrists though, and when I glance over at them I see the red welts rising up from my skin.

I swing myself off the bed and go over to the window, open it up a few inches on its latch to take out that oppressive stench of elderberries . . . that stench of Randolfo . . . and then I shift myself into the kitchen to see if I can find anything in the way of breakfast.

As I look about, I come across a clock. It's minimalist, and in a way reminds me of the clock in Brian's sitting room back at the mansion.

Again, with all things *style* it takes some brainpower to properly read it, since there are no numbers, and only chunky little marks.

I divine that it might be half past six in the morning.

For a moment I reflect on that.

I never was an earlier riser, but this morning, and *this* early, I actually feel quite switched on, what's the phrase: bright-eyed and bushy-tailed.

I dig out a transluscent container of granola from within one of the pine-wood cupboards, and a white—*square!*—porcelain bowl from another.

After a quick search, I locate the hidden-away fridge, and some milk within there. In addition to the milk, there's also half a dozen eggs, maybe a pound of butter, among other perishables.

I get the cereal down me, enjoying the *crunch* and the sweet taste in my mouth. Makes a nice change from blood, anyway, and then I turn my attention to the day ahead.

The first thing that strikes me, after I make the decision to take a shower, is that I don't have any clothes with me, other than the ones that I have on at the moment.

I pad my way back into the bedroom, curling my toes up in the thick, black carpet as I go. It really does feel like I'm walking across dog fur, or something like that.

I pick out a pine-wood dresser and I test out some of the drawers.

My clothes.

All here.

A slight tingle passes up my spine, and my stomach dips, because I know that someone has been in my room, and while I've been sleeping.

That they've pawed through my personal things, and then, admittedly with great care and attention, folded my clothes up and slotted them into these drawers.

I flip through my clothes all in there, vaguely hoping that they might've had some massive oversight and managed to leave *Solecito* in among them.

But, unsurprisingly, no luck there.

My next thought is that, perhaps, they've not separated my mobile from the rest of my things.

No luck there either, though.

I guess Randolfo takes great care in picking his goons.

I stand back from the dresser then peer out through the window. I see that there's a catch that will only allow it to be opened a few inches at a time. I won't be able to open it wide enough so that I might slip out, slither my way down a drainpipe . . . though I never was all that great at gymnastics . . . and, considering that, if I *do* manage to escape the castle grounds, I'll be the subject of a nationwide manhunt, it's most likely better just to drop the thing altogether.

That's right. My plan. I have to act natural, do the job Randolfo wants me to do, and then pick my moment to escape or, better, to bargain with him.

Because one thing's for certain, he's not going to keep me here a prisoner for the rest of my life.

I'd rather die.

* * *

All showered, and smelling of the sweet, rosemary-scented soap that's provided, with the lavender shampoo making my hair gleam more than I even want to contemplate, I hear a twin pair of knocks at the door.

"Come in," I say, lying on the bed, staring up at the ceiling, and just waiting to see what's going to happen today.

There's a *bleep-bleep* and then the lock mechanism whirrs.

The door creaks open on its hinges and I cast an uninterested glare over to it.

Standing there, in the doorway, is Germo.

Today he's back in his Big Boy suit, his green-tinted sunglasses tucked into his breast pocket. I see that his shoes are especially shiny today, and that it appears that he's had his black tie dry cleaned.

I guess you've got to dress for success.

He stands there, remaining stoic, his grey eyes unfeeling now—I can't believe that I *ever* saw anything in them at all. "Good morning," he says, and then, "you look quite nice."

I give him a faint smirk.

Today I'm wearing a light green blouse, and a pair of loose fitting black trousers. On my feet I have the same sensible pair of plimsolls. I get the impression that all this training with Viviana might just get a little active.

"Thanks," I say, "you look quite nice too."

It seems that the nuance either drifts over his head, or he chooses to ignore it, before he simply nods to me, lips pursed, and says, "Up, please."

I do as he says, and follow him down the corridor, and out of my bedroom.

Germo sets a mean pace, and though I know that I shouldn't even be entertaining the idea, I really can't help staring at his pair of buttocks, nestled there up against his tight-fitting suit trousers.

He really is all business today.

We head on through the castle, past more doors than I can count.

I guess that this whole top floor of the castle is all part of Randolfo's residence, because when we emerge out onto a balcony which sits out in the clean, fresh, mountain air, it's to meet with Viviana who's already up here.

I take a moment to breathe in the air. To cleanse my lungs of the stench of elderberries, and, now, that cologne of Germo's I've been forced to breathe while following on in his slipstream.

All about us, I can hear the birds tweeting in the trees, and the stir of leaves and branches. This whole place seems tranquil, a nice refuge from the overstated . . . well, *blackness* of the rest of the castle.

Beneath my feet, the floor is made up of the same sable shade as the rest of the place, though. Obsidian tiles. But, at least out here, there's a little light for contrast.

The morning sun beams down on me, and it feels like it's reenergising me, rather than sucking me of my energy as it seemed to yesterday, sitting down on the stone steps of the mansion and waiting for the results of Germo's faux search.

It makes me wonder if Señora Esmeralda died in the tumble down the slope. Because, if she didn't, then surely I might've had a chance to save her. She might well have been just injured, down there.

What sort of a scene would that have led to if Germo had come striding out of the house, *Solecito* down by his side, ready to finish the job.

Because, with a full night's sleep behind me, I think I can safely say that he tampered with Señora Esmeralda's car in some way . . . made it veer over to the right of the road just like that.

But that same fear remains.

That I might have been able to save her.

Today Viviana's wearing a deep purple tracksuit, along with a pair of brilliant-white trainers. Her blond-streaked black hair is done up in a neat bun at the back of her head. When she sees me, she gives me a dopey-eyed smile then advances. "Hello, Anna," she says. "Did you sleep well?"

"Wonderful," I say, keeping my tone dry.

Viviana glances off over my head and says something in Spanish, to Germo. It's a one-way conversation, and I watch the wrinkles break out about her eyes as she jibbers away at him. He remains unmoved, and then she shifts her focus back to me, gives a light sigh, then says, "Ridiculous, he will not leave us alone."

I look over at Germo.

Stone-faced.

Now he wears his green-tinted sunglasses.

Stands with his hands clasped at his belt buckle.

I shrug. "I guess he's worried about your safety, thinks that I'll try to take you hostage, or something."

Viviana rolls her eyes, and then she sets into Germo all over again. Obviously berating him about being there.

And all the while Germo doesn't offer so much as a raised eyebrow.

Seeing that this is getting nowhere, I decide that it might be time for me to step in. And so, setting my hand on my hip, I look over at him and say, "Señora Esmeralda, remember?"

He remains still. Hands still clutched at his belt buckle. But, this time, I see a very slight twitch, at the side of his face. He twists his neck round to Viviana, as if to ask her permission.

She assumes my own position, hand at hip and all, and shoots him one of her strongest of glares.

All of a sudden, Germo's resistance breaks, he looks over the two of us and then, it seems, out beyond us, before turning on his heel and returning into the main building of the castle.

"Nice work," Viviana says, and then, her voice slightly high-pitched, like an inquisitive child, "Who is Señora Esmeralda?"

CHAPTER TWENTY-FIVE

I **fob Viviana off** with an excuse about Señora Esmeralda, about it being something of a joke between me and Germo, and she seems to go for it. Though I've noticed, ever since the bullfight, really, that she acts differently around her father, in a way that makes me think both our goals might be mutually beneficial, I don't have any intention of nailing my colours to the mast.

Not just yet, anyway.

I look to her, take in her fresh, young girl's face. She's wearing light purple eye shadow to match her tracksuit.

Guess I'm not going to have to give her many lessons in coordination.

"So," she says, "where do we start?"

I look about the balcony. I see, nestled in the corner, there's an ominous-looking pale wooden crate. "What's in there?" I say.

She shifts over to the crate, and she bends down, sticks her bare fingers in beneath the gap at the lid, and then prises upwards.

I guess she loses hold of the lid at some point, because it drops onto the balcony tiles with a *slap*.

I take a few steps over to her and peer around her to the contents inside.

Straw. Lots of straw. Packing, I guess.

Viviana seems to know just what she's doing as she paws about inside the straw, and then removes what looks to be an extremely serviceable handgun.

A replica of *Solecito*, in fact.

I can tell it's not the same gun because, whereas *Solecito* is totally black, this pistol we've got here is a sleek chrome.

She clasps the grip and hands it to me, barrel pointed at my chest.

I clear my throat. "All right," I say. "First lesson, whenever you hand a gun to anyone you hold it like this"—I take it from her and show her, gripping it by the barrel, rather than the handle, and making sure that if it goes off it won't plant a bullet in anybody—"okay?"

She looks at me with wide, impressionable eyes, and I see that this— *all* this—is a little more than she bargained for, and I guess that she might be a little afraid by the whole thing.

Then again, if I was the daughter of a rich guy like Randolfo, and my father had enrolled me in self-defence lessons, I guess that I would feel just a touch apprehensive too.

"But it is not loaded," she says, nodding to the chrome gun.

"Yeah, but it's a good habit to get yourself into, believe me, it'll save you grief down the road."

"Grief?"

"Trouble. Problems. Bother."

"Ah," she says, mouth gaping open so I can get a good look at her tonsils and the uvula dangling about at the back of her throat.

"Good, so we're clear?"

She nods, vigorously.

"Fine, then show me."

"Show you what?"

I resist the temptation to give her a cuff round the ear, like a puppy that's piddled on the skirting board for the umpteenth time. Maybe I should've asked Germo for a newspaper before he skulked off. "How to pass the gun," I say, taking pity on her.

She does as I ask, all wide-eyed and open-mouthed, but, other than that, she does it just fine and I give her a pleasant smile by way of reward.

"Now," I say, "any ammunition in that crate?"

She turns back down to the crate. Rustles through the straw again before she straightens up with an armful of magazines.

I raise an eyebrow, thinking that Randolfo is really serious about her getting in some good practice with me.

I take one of the magazines off Viviana and I inspect it.

They're all blanks.

Of course they are.

Just because Randolfo is brutal doesn't mean that he's stupid.

Like a magician, I hold up the fresh magazine, watch the look of awe strike her face, and then, with a swift movement, I load it up into the pistol.

Snap it into place.

Then I cock the pistol.

I wait for the inevitable questions.

"And that is all?" she says, finally.

I nod.

She looks to the pistol in my hand, and then out beyond the balcony, to some of the trees before us, and I already know what's on her mind.

"I don't think your daddy's tenants would appreciate me shooting up on the roof here, do you think?"

She shrugs. "I do not think he cares. He said for us to train here."

I wait another second, wait for her to say something else, to run a little word of warning, something like that.

But I can see, from her nonchalant expression, that she's serious. That I *can* shoot off a few rounds from this balcony here.

And so, with a shrug of my own, I line up a shot on a tuft of grass five storeys below, and then let rip.

My ears ring long and hard before I remember that we've forgotten a pretty vital ingredient. I look back to Viviana to see that she's uncovered a pair of ear protectors from within that same crate, and she's holding one of the pairs out to me.

I take it from her with a slightly skittish smile, a little annoyed that, as the expert, I've been caught out. But she doesn't seem to notice . . . or, at least, she makes no remark about it, and it doesn't seem to register on her face either.

With the ear protectors fitted, I let off another shot.

And then another.

I love the smell. The smell that reminds me of battery acid. It brings me around. Makes me feel awake. I can feel that sting in my mouth, lolling over my tongue.

I feel every one of the shots as I squeeze the trigger. Brace myself for the kickback, keep the sight all lined up with my target. Using all the technique that I, too, was taught once.

Bang! Bang! Bang!

Shot after shot after shot.

They all pound into that poor, unsuspecting little tuft of grass down there, each time sending up a little puff of earth. And I never let that tuft of grass recover.

I just keep pounding it over and over again.

Until I've polished off the entire magazine, and then I look to Viviana, see that she's got the wide eyes out again, and the slightly parted lips. I can see the tip of her tongue, and the reflection of the sun on her saliva.

Her eyes—her *father's* eyes—slowly come up to meet mine, and I know just what she's going to ask next.

"Is it my turn?"

* * *

And so, for Monday's lesson, the *first* lesson, I have Viviana pump bullets into those tufts of grass down on the verge of the flower-beds. Though I give her a few well-chosen words of advice, just a little adjustment here and there in her posture, I have to admit that the girl has somewhat taken me by surprise.

Pleasant surprise.

Before I know it, the sun is high above our heads, and I can feel the unmistakable, prickly heat of midday all around us.

One thing that's good about being up here, in this castle, is that the humidity isn't so much of a factor, not like it was at Brian's mansion.

And the air smells so fresh. There's no dust lingering in it.

I wonder if Brian's ever considered making a swap with Randolfo: a castle for a mansion, even with me, someone who only looks in on a rich person's world, I know that Randolfo would never accept *that* trade.

Though I'd be just as happy with either the mansion or this castle.

Very happy in fact.

As I feel the sweat oozing out of me, and I smell the gentle, feminine smell of Viviana sweating too, I am on the cusp of suggesting that we head back inside for some shade.

Just for a little while.

But I'm forced to eat my words because a maid slinks out of the castle brandishing a parasol, which she plants into the black plastic base that I hadn't previously noticed.

Another maid appears too, but this one is somehow managing to lug a black plastic table and a pair of black plastic chairs.

Both maids set their loads down and then return to the castle just as quietly as they left it.

"Shall we sit?" Viviana says.

My muscles ache, but especially my wrists. And it feels like, with all the shooting I've been doing, that it's only served to give them more pain.

So I relish the break.

A few moments later yet *another* maid slinks out from the inside of the castle bearing a tray with sandwiches and a pair of tall, cool, ice-filled drinks. She lays the tray down on the table without so much as uttering a word, and then, with an elaborate curtsey—though, for me, *any* kind of curtsey is elaborate—she returns back into the castle, the same way the other two maids before her went.

I think about digging into the sandwiches and then recall my dual role of guest / slave, and so I look to Viviana for permission.

Thankfully, though, she's already tucking into the sandwiches, apparently not at all interested in what I'm getting up to with my own eating.

The sandwich turns out to be cheese and ham, and butter too, of course, all set in white bread. It feels like a little bit of a let down given all that I might've been led to expect from being kidnapped to a castle like this.

But the cheese and ham sandwiches do the job just fine, and only when I make serious inroads into no less than five of the sandwiches . . . there must be about twenty of them all laid out . . . and realise that Viviana is still picking away at her second—doing some kind of dissection ritual I'm sure my therapist, Julie, would be extremely interested in—do I see that I'm munching my way through these sandwiches a mite quick.

Then, just as quickly, I decide that, really I don't care.

I reach out for the drink laid out there. It's in a blue glass, but when I peer in I see that it's colourless. Water. I give it a sniff just to check, not wanting to find myself victim to something so commonplace as poison . . . though why Randolfo would go to all of this trouble simply to *poison* me escapes me for the time being.

The water's infused with lemon and lime, and, I think, a zest of tangerine too. Whatever it is they've put into this drink, it's absolutely delicious, and totally refreshing.

And, soon enough, drink finished, and eighth sandwich fully devoured, I decide that we're all ready for the afternoon session.

At the rate that Viviana is picking this stuff up, I wonder if I won't be able to hand her over to her father much earlier than expected.

Maybe if she gives a successful demonstration—or some other thing to measure my effectiveness as a teacher—and he sees that she's all ready, he'll let me loose after all.

. . . Not that I'm holding my breath.

Not a bit of it.

As I set Viviana up with the pistol again, and have her shooting at clumps of earth five storeys down, I'm dimly aware of the maids returning to collect together all the outdoor furniture, to take it back to wherever it came from.

For some reason, I glance back over my shoulder to see the maid that brought us the sandwiches on the tray.

I take in her pinstriped blue uniform, with its neat white apron hanging down the front. And the odd hairpiece she's wearing too. The one that looks like a hat some waitress in a diner might wear . . . and some maid from a hundred years ago might've worn.

She has an attractive, rounded jaw—an oval face—and extremely dark hair, slick with grease and hidden beneath that hat of hers.

She fixes me with her deep, dark brown eyes, and just stares at me for the longest time.

Only when another of the maid's arms appears out from the shadows of the castle, taps her on the arm, does she seem to snap out of her daze.

She blinks a couple of times, and then skitters back off into the castle, and I listen to her, and her co-workers', footsteps echo off along that marble floor.

I turn my attention back to Viviana, who is busying herself with the pistol, doing something that I can't quite fathom with the magazine.

I go over to help her and it seems that, somehow, she's managed to get it locked in place, the emptied magazine and all. I get it loose after a good minute's swearing and no small amount of sweat drooling down off my brow.

Finished, I hand it back to her. "There you go," I say. "Now you show me how to load it, okay?"

She nods slightly, picks up another magazine of blanks, and then, with a slight frown, and not-so-nimble fingers, manages to fit it to the pistol. To snap it into place.

She looks up at me, still as unsure as when she started, wanting my approval.

"Go on, then," I say. "Only one way to see if you've done it right, isn't there?"

Viviana clenches the grip of the pistol tight, and then heads off to the edge of the balcony. She leans up against the stone wall, lines up the shot, and then lets fly.

Looks like she did it just fine.

Once she's through with that magazine, I take the pistol back off her, and look out over the landscape which stretches out from us. To the squiggly roads and the cars rumbling along them like determined ants.

I guess lunch took a little longer than I thought, because, already, I can feel the strength of the sun ebbing away.

That ham and cheese sandwich sits great with my stomach and, for the first time in these rollercoaster twenty-four hours, I feel something approaching human.

Just breathing in this fresh air. Feeling that gentle, cooling breeze. With the aftertaste of lemon and lime, the hint of tangerine, just tingling away in my mouth.

As I'm looking the pistol over, checking that Viviana hasn't done any irreversible damage with her jamming the magazine, I feel a shadow cast over me.

My heart bucks, and blood flows to my skull.

Because my first thought is that Germo has returned.

But, when I look up, I see that, in fact, it's just Viviana.

She eyes me with those devastating, rosy brown irises of hers.

"You doing okay there?" I say.

Her eyes dart away from mine, and to look behind me. Over my head.

I look over there too.

This time Germo *is* standing there.

Just what sort of a snake in the grass *is* he?

All suited up, those tinted-green sunglasses bouncing sunlight directly into my eye. His hands clasped down at his belt buckle, as if he's waiting for something.

Perhaps he is.

Viviana leans into me and drops her voice to a whisper. "Wait for me," she says.

"What?"

She becomes fixated on Germo yet again, before giving me another tentative glance. "Tonight. Just . . . just." She meets my eye full on. "Just do not go to sleep."

I think about my answer. Realise that I want more information. But I see that she's already heading off to the crate, replacing the pistol inside, and the empty magazines too. And I realise that she has to go. That Germo standing there, lingering in the doorway to the balcony, means that playtime is over.

Whatever that means.

I watch her slip past Germo, standing at the opening, and then I move to follow.

Just as I brush past him, feel the silk fabric of his suit brush up against my bare arm, he reaches out and grabs hold of my wrist, and then says, in a low grumble, "You like to meet me tonight?"

I hold him in my gaze for a second or so. I can just about make out the outline of his eyes behind those green-tinted sunglasses, and then I say, "Do you really think I'm that stupid?"

He shoots me a smirk.

I shake off his hold and make a beeline for my bedroom, my mind already a flurry with just what Viviana wants to meet me for later on tonight.

CHAPTER TWENTY-SIX

I lie back on the bed. The moleskin spread tickling the back of my neck. TV on mute. The faint smell of butter lingering over everything—the residue of another of my pasta innovations . . . I think I cooked up the same thing back at Brian's mansion: boring, predictable, *me?*

Those rich, almost meaty, wads of pasta are still stuck between my teeth. I remember someone telling me once—AA?—that the key with cooking pasta is to get it just right.

Don't undercook or overcook, that was it.

And, I guess, since I've got it stuck in my teeth, I must've done one of the two.

But it did the trick with shutting my stomach up, so I guess that's the main thing.

Even though the TV's on mute, I can hear an odd sort of crackling, static sound passing through the air, seeming to tickle my eardrums, as if there's some transmission somewhere that if I was only to listen a little harder, I'd be able to decipher.

This time I have the TV switched to a music video channel. It's good to watch it right now because it keeps my mind alert, keeps my focus up. In a way it reminds me of muzzle flash. Reminds me of past times. Times that, with the help of a therapist, I've been trying my best to forget.

. . . No, that's not the way to put it . . . *resolve*, that's the way that Julie would say it.

If I shut my eyes, just for a moment, I can picture Julie, back there in her office.

I see her round glasses. Hair tumbling down to her shoulders.

Those *piercing* green eyes of hers.

And, of course, the fresh flowers that sit on the windowsill. I think about how they smell. How they make my nostrils tingle, and how, even though it's *my* session, and Julie constantly berates me for not making *my* feelings well known, I never say anything about them to her.

Never utter so much as a syllable that I might be in any discomfort at all.

I think about calling her now.

I have her number, of course, but it's . . . and then I remember, what with my status of 'prisoner,' I don't have access to my mobile phone, in fact I have no idea where it is.

And on reflection I suppose that getting my brain picked over shouldn't really be heading my priority list right at the moment.

Escape should be the foremost thing on my mind.

And, for that, I'll need to be practical. To think things through properly. To *keep* my brain together so I don't make any obvious, giveaway mistakes.

I watch the twenty-something bands of boys come and go, their images flicker onto the screen, their angst-ridden faces, and their smudged-up black makeup.

Their ridiculously spiked hair.

Do they really think that's what the girls go for?

Are girls really the ones that they're trying to impress?

Well, and I'll tell you this for nothing, these boys are doing nothing for the female, mid-thirties crowd.

Several times I catch myself drifting off, allowing that gentle static crackle to act as a lullaby, and wish me away to the Land of Nod.

But, each time, I manage to catch a hold of myself, and I sweep off those feelings of drowsiness.

In the end, I come to a more practical solution to the problem, and prop myself up in bed—upright, it seems, there's much less risk of me snoring on my midnight caller.

Despite these stauncher attempts to keep myself awake, it's only when I hear the low mumble of a male voice, outside my bedroom door, that I fully snap back to consciousness.

Funny, I hadn't reasoned before that there would be someone standing sentry outside my door, but, thinking about it now, I suppose that it makes sense.

I am a prisoner, after all.

I listen to the conversation for what it's worth since I have no hope of working out what they're saying in Spanish outside, and I just wait there, back pressed up against the headboard seeing where I'm going to fit in with this discussion.

I estimate it to be about a minute later when I hear the mechanism on my door go *bleep-bleep*, and then the lock go *whirr*, before I observe Viviana's slender frame slipping in round the edge.

She's dressed in a nightie, a light pink silk affair, and I wonder if she makes a habit of skipping about the castle at night in it. Because, one thing's for sure, with all these red-blooded males bobbing about, she's certainly braver than I am.

At least without a gun in her hand.

She has nothing on her feet, and her hair hangs freely now.

I look to her slender ankles and think about how they're almost facsimiles of her wrists. Spindly, and delicate. Just ripe for getting broken with a misplaced step here or there.

Her face is stripped of makeup and that, along with the nightie, makes her seem several years younger to me, though I'm certain that I've pinned her right as being in her early twenties.

She glances back over her shoulder, and we both watch the door swing shut with a *slap*, and the *buzz* of the lock mechanism kick back in. Another pair of bleeps, and I know that the two of us are locked into my bedroom now.

Everything's set for the slumber party.

Viviana sniffs at the air, wrinkling up her nose in a way that reminds me of a baby rabbit. "Pasta?" she says.

I nod.

"Smells nice."

I give her a smile this time and will her into getting on with getting *out* whatever it is that she's going to say. I have to admit, following the previous comatose hours, I just want to prise myself in between the sheets and get a decent eight hours' sleep.

She settles down on the bed beside me, and she brings her bare foot up onto the mattress, begins to play with her toenails—again, like a much younger girl, and it makes me wonder just how much exposure she's had to the Big Bad World outside of these castle walls.

Daddy sent her to meet me alone, so I guess that's a pretty good start.

As she picks at her toenails, I give a yawn and then decide, for both our sakes, that I'm better off being direct with her. "All right," I say, "what's the big secret?"

She stops picking at her toenails, stares off at the thick, curly carpet, and then, flicking her brushed hair over her shoulder, she meets me with those rosy brown eyes. "It is something I have heard."

"Yeah? And what's that?"

She presses her lips together. Squeezes all the blood out of them. They go almost green from the effort she puts into the action.

"Wouldn't your daddy be pissed off about you sneaking off to have private conversations with me in the middle of the night?"

She smirks, and it seems to loosen her tongue. "If my father knew what I know then he would probably not let me out of my room."

I have to admit that now I'm intrigued. "And what's that?"

She looks away from me, stares into mid air, and clasps one of her bare feet with her hand. With that fragile, pale hand. "I think I know the reason," she says, "the reason why my father wants me to be trained by you."

I watch her Adam's apple bob in her throat, and I see that her skin is all broken out in goose bumps.

"One night, when I was coming back home late at night, many weeks ago, I could hear some talking. Coming from my father's penthouse. And, well, it is strange, because my father, he usually is alone in the evenings. He likes to be alone."

I think about interjecting something about my knowledge of men—especially *single* men, as I assume Randolfo to be—but I hold back.

Mostly because of the way her voice wavers and how she is trembling. Now doesn't seem like the time to make jokes.

"I think that was why I knew I had to go and investigate. And so, instead of going to my own apartment, I followed the voices, and I stood in the reception area to my father's penthouse. And I waited."

"What did you hear?"

She screws up her features, almost in a scowl. "He was speaking with a man about . . . about," she pauses and I get the urge to reach out and shake the words from her, but, again, Common Sense, Practical Anna intervenes and I hold myself back, "about *me*."

I listen to that final word linger in the air, and think about the stress she's put on it.

But I only get so long to do that before she breaks out in heaving sobs, and collapses into my chest.

* * *

Not really sure what's wrong with me, but I've never been all that good with criers.

From top to bottom, I never know what to tell them, what to do—to hug them, or to be all standoffish—or if I should simply make quiet, hushing noises like I used to do when one of my kids would get up bawling in the night.

That always seemed to work well with babies.

But with adults, not so much.

Still, in this situation, I trust my gut instinct of throwing my arms about the crying girl, and pulling her into my t-shirt, more to drown out her sobs than anything else.

Because one thing that I can't afford is her drawing the attention of the guard outside, and him coming moseying in here, prying about, insisting that he take Viviana back to bed.

And she can't go to bed, not till she's told me this secret of hers.

I feel her tears soaking into my t-shirt, and I can feel her shudders growing more and more intense. I notice that she's taken hold of a scrap of my t-shirt in her fist, and that she holds it extremely tight, so tight that she's squeezing the blood out of her hand.

I breathe her in, the remnants of her peachy perfume still there despite the overriding scent of the bath salts.

In a giddy moment, I think about how I haven't taken advantage of the bath here yet, and make a note, before I check out of this room, that I should do so.

When I feel her sobbing subsiding, and the tension in her muscles relaxing, I bring her back up from my chest, and make eye contact with her again.

When I speak, I'm a little taken aback that I manage to keep my tone so measured, and even a little bit *soft*. If I'm not careful maybe one of these days I'll turn into a softy.

And wouldn't that be a travesty for my occupation.

Her eyelids droop and I can see now that there are red veins ribbing her eyes, and I wonder whether she's been sleeping well.

"You've gotta tell me," I say. "Otherwise how am I going to help?"

She shakes her head. "No, Anna, you cannot help me, no one can help me now."

"Then what's the point of you coming here, of you telling me your secret?"

Her shoulders rise and fall in gentle motion as she takes heady breaths, slowly getting her heart rate, and all the rest of her body, back under control.

Maybe I should think of a shift in profession to a therapist . . . I'm sure that Julie would laugh about that one, after I'd taken a good dozen or so steps out the door first, though, of course.

"Because," Viviana says, "there's a good chance that you can save yourself, Anna, that is the most important now."

She rises up, headed for the door, trying to get away from me before she's told the full story.

Not on my watch.

I grab hold of her nightie, maybe a little too roughly, and drag her back down onto the bed beside me. Once more our eyes meet. "No," I say. "You tell me everything that's going on, and you tell me about it now, that clear?"

Her bottom lip wobbles just a little, but, in the end, she gives me a doleful nod. After a moment or two, she continues on. "I do not know the exact nature of the plan, I must admit, but I do know that my father, that he intends to . . ." her voice wavers again, filling with tears, but she holds them back ". . . I mean, he plans to give me to an associate, the one who was visiting the night before. I . . . I do not know, but from the way it sounded, his meeting with the man, it sounded like my father has troubles."

"Troubles?"

"Yes, he has troubles, I do not know exactly, but he wanted the deal to be that he would give this man . . . give this man, *me*."

I screw up my eyes, and wonder just what sort of a deal this is supposed to be. But, then, everything just seems to slip into place, and I manage to get it all sorted out in my mind. To make sense of it all.

Sometimes I worry for my sanity, seeing as I seem to have this knack for being able to see into the inner workings of psychopaths' master plans.

I manage to raise a slight smile. "That's why he wants you to go through this training," I say, "when he plans to trade you to this man, for whatever reason, he's planning on giving you a gun so that you can fight back—so that you can break your way out of there."

She glares at me. "I do not follow you."

"Don't you see? That's why your father's put on all this security for me, he's somehow got it into his head that I'm some sort of expert troublemaker, that I know how to get myself out of just about any situation. Can find a way of extricating myself. And he believes that so much that he had to lay on an . . . an—"

And then I realise that I haven't let slip to Viviana about Señora Esmeralda . . . but I figure that, since she's been so frank with me, and I have no reason *not* to believe her story about her father's maniacal plotting . . . I mean, what other type of person would go to all the trouble that she's gone to for me?

So I decide to tell her.

She sits still while I go through my end of things, bring her up to date with just about everything, and she listens on in a kind of locked-down daze, so much so that I'm not certain that she's taking all the information in.

But, I realise that she has when she speaks again.

"Terrible," she says. "What must you think of my father."

I raise my eyebrows. "What must *you* think about your father?"

She gives me a narrow, sidelong smile. "Well, what else? He is my father, I have no choice, I love him, whatever it is that he decides to do with me. I cannot change that."

Though I can't say I've ever been in Viviana's position, I don't think that I'd be able to admit the same thing. If it was me, I'd have been out of there in a shot . . . though, thinking about the level of security Randolfo's running about his castle, I wonder just how realistic that really is: especially for someone as apparently harmless as Viviana.

Viviana reaches out and takes my hand in hers, interlocks her dainty fingers with my much more beaten-up ones and says, "Anna, that was not all that I heard. I stood there for a long time to listen, and I heard about the arrangements for the exchange."

"Go on."

"Well, at first, it was planned for a few months from now, but I suppose that my father has had problems, because he brought you here sooner, and he did those . . . those *terrible* things to get you to come at all."

"Let's make no bones about it, he *forced* me to come. I really have no alternative."

She nods. "Yes, Anna, that is true, and I am very sorry about it. But, for now, we must live with the circumstances." She sniffs a little, and reaches up to wipe away a lingering tear from her cheek. "My father, they agreed for the exchange to happen not too far from here, to happen near a bridge which is known as Puente de los Duendes."

"'Pwentay,' what?"

"It means, more or less, The Bridge of the Goblins."

"Okay."

"Yes, and that is the place where they want to change me, to give me to the contact of my father, whoever he might be."

"And what did you mean about it being a chance for me to escape?"

"Right, yes, well, the way that I see it, if you wish to escape, then that will be the perfect day, when they take me away. Because, I heard my father speaking on the phone a little while later, making plans with Germo, and the other guards. They will all be going. They will leave you here alone."

I think this over. Try to get it straight.

What Viviana's proposing is extremely noble, and not a little crazy. She really is floating the possibility of her falling into great, unknowable danger, as being a mere diversion for me.

I guess that's what you call altruism in its purest form.

At least I know that it'd never pop into my head to consider such a thing.

But, then again, I guess that I'm me.

"When?" I say.

"Hmm," she replies, with a shake of the head. "I do not know." She brightens her tone, just a touch. "But I shall find a way to tell you when the day arrives, do not worry and, until then, we shall continue the training, just as planned. And then the day they take me, that is the day that you must get away."

We sit stewing in silence for a long while, neither of us with anything else to add to the conversation. What *could* either of us possibly add to the conversation?

After a little while, Viviana leans forwards and I take her in a firm hug, and then she pads her way barefooted out of my room, and all is still again.

As I sit there, on the edge of my bed, the thing that surprises me the most is the anger. The anger that's stirring deep within me.

And the unshakable knowledge that no way in *hell* am I going to allow them to take Viviana away.

Not on my watch.

CHAPTER TWENTY-SEVEN

Just as planned, over the next few weeks, neither of us give anything away. Though, it's not all that hard considering that I don't see Randolfo about the castle that much.

I *do* see Germo, however.

I see him around *a lot.*

And, to be honest, it bugs the hell out of me.

But there's nothing I can do, because until I'm outside of his sphere of influence I have to put up with his leering, smirking looks . . . and those bulging muscles bursting out from his suit too.

He knows attraction when he sees it, and he's not afraid of being a real tease.

Not that I've got *any* intention of getting my lips caught on one of those barbs.

I think that I sink myself deeper into my classes with Viviana, really try and show her just how to be like me. How to use a gun like me. And I feel like she makes real progress throughout our many hours together.

In fact, I'd go as far to say that she has a pure streak of raw talent . . . and it's not often that you see that in a petite girl like her, an *unassuming* girl like her.

We spend a bunch of time on running, us thrashing it out through the expansive grounds of the castle, never going beyond the walls. And when we come across a forest, why, that's just the perfect place for us to practise a little gymnastics.

To show her how she might get herself out of a tight spot . . . or two.

And it all comes down to today. All of it building up.

Now, together, her firing off round after round into clumps of earth from the fifth-floor balcony, and me leaning up against the wall, in the shade, making a comment every so often.

It seems like we've been like this for decades. Been friends for decades.

Master and apprentice.

I can't seem to get my mind off the lecherous *Germo* skulking about behind us. In that black suit, that black *tie* of his, always in that same pose, keeping his hands clutched at his belt buckle.

I wonder if he thinks he could beat me in a straight gun battle. If it was just me and him, both of us armed with pistols.

I know who *I'd* put my money on, because if there's anything I've learned about a man who needs backup, and to have everyone with him—himself included—packing a semi-automatic rifle, it's that he really doesn't have all that much confidence in his own marksmanship.

Except when it comes to popping one between the eyes of an old lady who's just suffered a car crash. That comes *really* natural to him.

But I lay my own personal feelings to one side, and just keep on concentrating on Viviana, and getting her to shoot straight, and to load up her gun quickly . . . because I want her to be able to take care of whatever scumbag comes to pick her up without trouble.

As if it's instinct.

I want her to be *that* well-oiled and *that* deadly.

And it all comes down to this afternoon, just after I've watched Viviana load five successive magazines into her pistol with flawless accuracy and then shoot off at the vague spot in the flowerbed I pointed too.

Again, *flawless*.

I think that I notice the difference with Germo, he's fidgetier, which is to say that he is fidgeting *at all*. Every time I turn around to take a look over him—I haven't been able to quite shake the deadly fantasies of him rocking up behind me with a rifle, for some reason—I see him buttoning and unbuttoning the cuffs of his suit jacket.

And then, a couple of other times, adjusting his already perfectly balanced sunglasses over the ridge of his nose.

That puts me on edge.

But I try my best not to let it show to Viviana, I just give her the normal words of encouragement, and the general tips I've been dishing out for weeks now, and which she has found her way to mastering completely.

At least I'm safe in the knowledge that I've done my best.

As Vivian empties a sixth magazine, I hear a slow clapping above my head, and when I turn, shrug off my ear protectors, I see Randolfo himself, in all his smug glory, standing above us, looking out from a window which I guess forms another part of his penthouse.

He looks down on me with a vague smile, and says, "It looks like you have taught her very well. I am very impressed."

But I know that he sounds far more *smug* than impressed.

People like Randolfo I've dealt with my entire life. They're the ones . . . the bosses, those higher up in the chains of command . . . who think that because *they* picked out the talent that everything said talent accomplishes is down to them.

Not that he would understand the true worth of dedication and practice.

And *I'm* certainly not the one to instil those virtues in him.

Not without a gun in my hand, in any case.

Viviana looks to me, her instructor, for a cue on what to do next.

I give her a simple nod, though what I really want to do is run to her and grab a hold of her and spin her round in ever-increasing circles. Because what she's achieved in this short space of time, the level of proficiency she has managed to achieve . . . well, there are some who don't manage to achieve it after years and years of blood and sweat . . . and I *do* mean blood.

She gives the slightest twitch of a smile, and then heads back to the crate, to replace the pistol there.

But her father—Randolfo—calls out from above in Spanish to her, and she pulls up, doesn't replace the pistol in the crate after all.

He looks down at me for a final time, gives me a nod, and a brief smile, then returns from whence he came.

I look back to Germo, who has stopped his fidgeting in the presence of his boss, and is now turned on his side, waiting for us to re-enter the castle.

I glance to Viviana, see the pistol still clutched in her grip, and we *both* know just what's going on. We know that soon they will be taking Viviana out to be exchanged.

To be given away to another man, like an *animal*.

I wait for Viviana to brush past me, before heading on after her, into the hallway, and down the corridor.

I can hear Germo's hard, sure footsteps already echoing about, and I guess my mind's on other things when I feel their arms on me.

The other guards.

They seize hold of my arms, their palms all blistered and weathered from their work, and I feel them tweak my wrists down and then the familiar scratch of the cable ties as they bind my hands again.

My heart pounds hard. And I feel sweat begin to well out of me again. In my stomach, I feel a nauseous swill, and I bite down hard on my tongue to stop my mind from breaking free. To stop myself from fainting.

Because I still have work to do.

I'm sure there's something I can still do for Viviana . . . if I can just . . .

I yank back my leg, and kick hard, catching one of the men right in the shinbone.

I hear his grunt of pain, but there's no snap of bone, and I know, right then, that I've lost it. I've lost the upper hand of surprise. Because now, from now on, they'll keep such a close eye on me. They realise that my spirit wasn't broken at all. That I was just biding my time.

Though I fight back some more, manage to catch the other one in the crotch with the toe of my shoe, I know that the fight is lost.

And, soon enough, they shove me down onto the marble floor, press my cheek up against the cool surface, and I feel the cable ties digging into my supple skin once more.

I guess, this time, I'm just going to have to sit this out.

But I tried my best.

And I hope, from the bottom of my heart, that Viviana *can* resist.

Stand up for herself.

No . . . I'm *sure* that she can.

I'm not quite sure exactly what I expect following the guards slapping the cable ties back onto my wrists, reopening those only recently healed scars, and grabbing a hold of me: treating me like some ragdoll.

Maybe I thought they'd just be satisfied with leading me back to my room. Maybe, in my wildest dreams, I could see them hurling me inside, cable ties still binding my wrist, and then slamming the door.

What I *didn't* expect, however, was for them to lead me back through the castle, back along all those jet-black marble floors, and to the service lift.

Right away, I surmise that this means me going off with them . . . me going off to this exchange.

Who knows what wild and bone-headed ideas Randolfo has in mind.

Maybe he's going to try and pass me off as his daughter.

Or maybe he's going to try and throw me in as a bonus.

. . . Well, and he should know it well now, *this* bonus has claws.

I look out ahead, to the backs of Germo's heels, as we all get into the lift. I decide the time's right to save my energy and so I stop struggling.

If they really are going to take me off with them, to the exchange point, then things are truly better than I expected. At least I'll have a much better chance of saving Viviana out there, instead of being cooped up in my bedroom.

The lift shudders a little as we descend, swooping down those levels to the underground car park below. Or, at least, that's where I believe we're headed.

I see Germo dip into his pocket, and remove a black cloth. He looks to the guards, and then peers down at me, before taking a step forward, and draping the cloth down over my eyes.

Everything goes black.

I feel the lift come to a halt.

I breathe in expecting the underground car park, to smell that cement scent coming at me from all angles. But, no . . . that stench of elderberries still dominates *everything*.

One of the guards prods me in the back, I stumble forward. I want to hold my arms out, to check my surroundings, so that I don't slip and break something.

I wait, heart tickling at my throat, and then, with a solid, yet almost distant, *thwack!* I feel myself dropping down.

And the swill of unconsciousness overwhelming me.
A purple haze descending over my eyes.
Then the blackness is truly complete.

CHAPTER TWENTY-EIGHT

Steam smothers my mouth. Tickles my cheeks. It's warm, and moist, and thick in the air. It's hard to breathe. Really hard. My heart lollops as if caught in a stupor. And then picks up. Quicker. Taps out faster.

Ba-dum. Ba-dum. Ba-dum.

Faster still.

BA-dum. BA-dum. BA-dum.

Even faster.

BA-DUM. BA-DUM. BA-DUM.

It's like my heart beats away against my body. Trying to *escape* my body.

An almost impossibly acute, *searing* pain strikes my right temple.

I try to move my hand upwards, to touch the pain. But I can't. My hands are still bound. Tied up with the cable ties. Behind my back.

I shift my weight. Realise the surface beneath me is soft. Materials. Bed sheets. Towels.

Though my eyes are open wide, everything is black. Then I remember the blindfold. Germo's parting gift to me.

Along with that punch.

Slowly I feel my brain prickling at the inside of my skull. The steady drip of adrenalin re-enter my veins. And my breathing follows.

Becomes shallower. My heart more frantic.

The taste of blood in my mouth more pronounced.

I breathe in again. Just that moist air. That *steam*. All around me. Crushing down on me, like a thundercloud.

In the near distance I can hear machinery churning. The gentle pounding and scraping.

And then I realise it's drawing closer.

The sound is growing louder.

I'm on a conveyor belt. What else could it be? And I'm moving along it with jerky little motions.

In this industrial-sized laundry container.

And I know just what Germo has planned for me. Where he's had me left. Just what's going to happen to me if I don't manage to extricate myself from this.

I'll be burned alive in the machinery, if nothing else.

But maybe that's his intention.

I guess it's a much trickier thing to have someone killed than to leave them with some visible scars. Scars that'll make them think twice next time.

Though I always *was* a slow leaner.

Before I really think of it, I find myself shouting out.

"Help! Help!"

Even as I listen to my words rumble out from between my lips, I can tell that they're lost in the industry of the machines. And that there's no chance anyone will be able to hear.

But I have to try.

"Help!"

Can I hear footsteps? Someone making their way towards me? A muttered conversation perhaps?

Most likely it's just the grinding of the machines. My hypersensitive brain trying to make some sense of that deeply *unhuman* scraping and thrashing. And the constant steam that just seems to billow at me from everywhere.

"Help!"

This time I'm certain I hear voices. One-hundred-per-cent sure of it.

And yet, some other voice within my mind tells me that I'm going crazy. That I'm as good as dead.

The steam's hotter now. It feels like I'm holding my head over a boiling kettle. Feeling the froth and foam of the scalding steam blow up at my cheeks.

"Help!"

All at once, I hear it. The gentle, fading sound of the machines. The scraping and the thrashing, and the puffs of steam slowing down and then coming to a standstill.

The air grows colder. At least not enough to be scalding any longer.

My heart slows, and I feel my muscles loosen.

I can relax now.

I tell myself I can relax.

Someone has punched the Stop button.

The voices outside get louder. I listen into them jabbering away. I try to make out something. Something that I can understand. My brain warps their words, seems to make inroads into understanding just what they're saying . . . but loses it just as quickly.

And I curse myself for not having brought so much as a bilingual dictionary with me on holiday. But who was to know that I'd actually run into real, living, breathing Spaniards on this trip? I was supposed to just veg out in Brian's mansion.

Guess this is quite a long way from Brian's mansion now.

More muttering. I guess they're having some sort of argument.

A tingle passes through my bloodstream, and I know that I've got to ensure that I get out of here. I have to make sure they know I'm here.

And so I call out again, this time louder than all the others, "HELP!"

* * *

The conversation falls to a hush, and I know that they've definitely heard me. That they know that I'm here. So they have to let me out now.

Don't they?

Or has Germo got them under orders too?

Has he made them complicit in his plan to have me boiled alive along with the castle's laundry?

I don't imagine it'll do wonders for the linen.

I hear clanging. All about me. No more talking now.

And then a much louder clang, and, through my blindfold, I can see that it's got lighter out. A rush of fresh air hits me. It feels cool as ice. And I breathe it in, only realising now just how stifling the air all around me really was.

A tentative hand reaches out. Touches me. Hard fingertips. Fingertips that I guess have been hardened from a life of working with all sorts of industrial-strength bleaches and soaps, and whatever else.

Those fingertips are gentle, though, and they carefully work at my blindfold, the finger finding its way beneath the material, and prising it up, off my face.

Gradually, I feel the blindfold slacken off. And then fall away.

It slips down to my neck.

For a second the light is overwhelming. I screw up my eyes against it. I feel my right temple pounding hard. A dizziness catches me.

When I get up the bravery to fully open my eyes, I see three women looking down at me.

They're all wearing the same uniform, that maid's uniform:

Blue pinstripes, a neat white apron, and that papery hat that looks like the ones that old-style diner waitresses would wear.

I realise that all three of them are the same maids that I saw almost every day up on the balcony, the ones that brought us the refreshments.

And then I recognise the one closest to me, the one that tore the blindfold off, the one with the rounded jaw, oval face and dark hair. An attractive lady maybe a few years under thirty.

Just about manage to get out an exasperated, "Gracias," before they all crowd around me to help me out of this laundry hamper.

* * *

The maids all stand back from me in a way that reminds me of frightened cattle. They all have those same handsome deep brown eyes, and about the same deeply tanned complexion.

A complexion that reminds me a touch of Randolfo.

But I shake that memory away as quickly as I can.

At first, as I stand back up on my feet, I feel a little wobbly. I stumble from one side to the other before I finally get a handle on how to stand still.

My brain still throbs. My mouth still tastes of blood. And I know that I'm flushed all over still from the steam.

I glance back at the thing I was inside.

It's a metal chamber that runs about the length of the room, perhaps about fifty feet long in all, and I see that there are hatches along the way . . . and, a little further on down, a large, and extremely ominous-looking, large chamber.

I know that's where most of the *deep* cleaning gets done.

And I can just tell it wouldn't have done me any good to find myself inside it.

I shake off my daze and show the maids my hands, still bound behind my back.

They all just stare back at me, apparently not knowing what to do.

"Scissors?" I say. "A knife?"

Still no response.

Round eyes all round.

I look to the maid that stopped and stared at me that day on the balcony, wiggle my hands in her direction, and she seems to get the hint.

In any case, she waddles off across the cream-tiled floor, and over to the other side of the room. When she returns she's carrying a pair of what look like sheers. I guess it's what they use for cutting material down here, for making alterations.

I turn and shut my eyes, hoping that she's not going to get all twitchy on me, that she's not going to start trembling all over. But she's sure, and her aim is true with the shears, and she lets me loose of the cable ties.

I bring my hands round and, straight away, reach up to touch my right temple.

There's a throbbing great welt there. As I press my fingers up against it, I can feel my pulse pounding away inside of its mass.

It's like someone's transplanted a golf ball onto my forehead.

I make a promise to myself that, next time I see Germo, I'm going to have to hit him just as hard.

If not just a little harder . . . so that he'll learn his lesson and all.

I bring my hand back down, still wincing with those little stabs of pain that continue on for a few more seconds from where I've touched the welt.

Then I turn my attention back to the situation.

Viviana.

I need to help Viviana.

I think about what she said, how Randolfo was planning on taking Germo and the other two guards along with him today. I know that it'll mean that I'm here alone . . . just as Viviana told me I would be before. And I bet I can guess just where Randolfo keeps the gun . . . *my* gun.

My Little Sun.

I turn to the maids then slow myself down, reminding myself that they can't speak English.

Or can they?

Only one way to find out.

"English?" I say. "Any of you speak English?"

I wait for a moment, all the maids still locking me with stone-faced, wide-eyed stares, and then the maid, the one that stared at me that time up on the balcony speaks up.

"Yes," she says. "I speak little."

CHAPTER TWENTY-NINE

Though I feel a little bad about implicating the maid in anything that might mean trouble for her later with her boss—with *Señor* Randolfo—I tell myself that it's for the greater good.

That my main priority right now needs to be to intercept this exchange, to get to Viviana as quickly as I possibly can.

I grip on tight to the maid's wrist, and I can hear her footsteps skittering along behind mine as she struggles to keep up. She's a good half a foot shorter than me so she probably needs two steps for every one of my own.

That stench of elderberries seems to get riper and riper in my nostrils as we draw closer to Randolfo's penthouse, and I flip a glance to the lady in the lobby, back up on the fifth floor, but she turns back to her work, apparently blissfully ignorant of all the kidnapping and backstabbing and attempted murder that's going on around here.

The bloody taste in my mouth gets too much to bear and I swallow several times, doing my best to get shot of it. But to no effect.

It's only then that I realise that what I pinned before as being blood is really the dewy taste of the steam.

Funny how close blood can come to water sometimes.

As we draw into the vacated reception area of Randolfo's apartment, I eye up the fingerprint scanner there. Its angry little red LED glaring up at us.

And I really hope that Randolfo's gone now.

That *all* of them have headed out to the exchange.

Because if he *has* left a guard behind then I'll have to kill him.

I look to the maid, the poor lady that saved me, and that I've tugged along behind me with only a hurried explanation in English, that I'm not sure she even understood.

Still, she hasn't struggled to get away, and seems to have just gone with the flow of all this. So I hope that she's on my side.

I look to her now, see her still looking at me with those wide eyes. "Can you let me in here? Have you got some way of letting me in?"

"In?" she says, wrinkles appearing in her forehead, and the first flush of tears appearing in her eyes.

"Yes," I say. "*In. In.* I have to get *in* here right now!"

Only when I hear my voice coming back at me off the walls of the corridor do I realise that I've been shouting at her.

She flinches a little just as I let up on my berating.

As if half-stuck by a daze, she reaches down to her white apron, and then beneath it, to a pocket I guess she keeps there in her skirt.

I hear a slight *tinkle* of keys, and then see that she's brought out a scuffed-up, white plastic card. She looks me in the eye, still seemingly one solid shove from tears, and then says, "With permission, please."

I step back.

She brings the card up to that glowering red LED light, and I listen for the *bleep-bleep*—that *wonderful* sound!—and I see the red light turn green. And hear the locking mechanism disengage.

Being as gentle as my rapidly beating heart will allow, I slip past her and into Randolfo's apartment.

$$* * *$$

I take in Randolfo's apartment for the second time, this time under only a little less duress than the first.

The moleskin sofa. The mahogany coffee table. The plasma TV.

I have to be quick. I know that.

I step over the thick, curly black carpet, stumbling a few times as I combat the last remnants of the nausea that Germo knocked into me with that punch to my right temple.

I look about the place. Size it up. Try and peel back the facades to see just where Randolfo has *Solecito* hidden. If it's even here at all.

After my first five minutes of looking, of pawing through every single drawer in the sitting room and finding nothing, I decide, looking down the corridor to the rest of the apartment and seeing that there must be a dozen more rooms to check, that it might be worthwhile examining my strategy a little.

Revaluating.

I look to the maid who is bobbing about by the front door of the apartment, still, as if Randolfo might arrive back home at any moment . . . and, I tell myself, as far as *I* know he just might.

I have no way of knowing just how long I've been knocked out. How long I was lying in that laundry hamper before waking up.

I approach her, clearly frightening her with what must be my flushed-up face from the steam, and that enormous great welt sticking out of my forehead. "Gun," I say. "I'm looking for a gun. Do you know where I might find one?"

Her eyes appear to shake in their sockets, and her bottom lip trembles. Just when I'm sure she's about to crumple up on herself and break out into inconsolable sobs, she nods firmly, and then, with several quick steps over the carpet—as if she's walking on hot coals—she leads me along the corridor, and to the penultimate room along.

She pauses a moment in the doorway and then, with a quick glance back at me, maybe looking for reassurance, she pads inside.

* * *

The maid flips on the light, casting a gentle, bluish glow over the room.

An enormous painting of the sea dominates the wall opposite the window. And it takes me just a moment to sketch that coastline, and to deduce that it's the beach at San Floriano.

The day is sunny, and there're several families—blurry multi-coloured dots—swarming the beach. Striped umbrellas. And the promenade is awash with activity.

I study the beachfront, try to see if I can make out the *Por La Playa* bar, but no luck.

Either the painter took some liberties with his art, or the bar didn't exist when he painted it.

I think a little about those cool, soothing lime drinks the barman poured, and the days I spent down on the beach. The others I spent there paddling about in the sea. And, I have to admit, that seems a more naïve time now . . . a time when I thought that I'd really got away.

But I never had, not really.

Germo was always there.

Always *watching*.

I turn my attention back to the maid who's sweeping through a filing cabinet. It's black metal to match the carpet and the general décor of the castle. And, as she flips through it, I can smell that sharp scent of glue in the air.

When I go over, and take a glance over her shoulder, I see that the filing cabinet is filled with photos. Though I don't get much of a chance to look at any particulars, I can recognise the smiling faces there.

That the young girl—getting older with each of the maid's flips, it seems—is Viviana.

And that bronzed-up, gurning, scumbag beside her is, of course, her father.

Randolfo.

The maid stops. She glances back over her shoulder. Eyes alert now. No sign of any impending tears now. She stands back, lips slightly parted, waiting for me to make the next move.

At first I'm not sure what she means, I can't see the gun anywhere. Not in the filing cabinet. And then I engage my brain, I reach deep into the filing cabinet, my bare arm brushing the tops of the cardboard dividers, and then I dip down right to the back of the unit, and brush a plastic bag.

I brush it with my fingertips a couple more times. And, even though the plastic gets in the way, I can feel the rugged surface of the grip nestled within.

The gun. I'm sure of it.

But I can only brush at the bag. It seems impossible for me to get a good grip on it.

I look back to the maid, as if silently imploring guidance from her, and I have the luck of having stumbled across a lady of solid intuition, because she waves me back, takes a hold of the drawer, and then heaves it up and off its runners.

She plonks it down on the floor, sending the cardboard divides jiggling, and a few of the photos flashing up at me for too short a time for me to take stock of them.

I glance to the back of the drawer, see the pistol there, wrapped inside a clear plastic bag, and see the brown industrial tape that keeps it firmly in place.

I get it loose with a solid *rip*, and then tear open the plastic bag.

I'm already halfway through checking *Solecito* over, whipping out the magazine, checking it's loaded—it is—before I think to look over to the maid.

To see just what she's up to.

And, of course, her face is contorted in fear.

I realise that while I've been checking over the gun, I've placed myself between her and the door, and to the uninformed observer . . . or to someone who really has no handle on just what I'm up to—the full *context* of what I'm up to—I guess that it might come across as somewhat threatening.

As if to neutralise this, or to counteract it, I give the maid an easy smile, and then lock the magazine back into *Solecito*.

She gives me a faint smile back, but falls short of hurrying forwards to embrace me.

I don't blame her. I'm sure I look a right nut what with the bulging welt on my forehead and this pistol in my hand. And I bet the maid's wondering just what got into her mind to bring me up here in the first place.

I decide that there's no time to waste, and I turn to leave Randolfo's apartment, only for the maid to break her silence.

"You bring her back, yes?"

I halt, do a half turn and look back to her. Taking care to keep the pistol down at my thigh, pointed to the ugly, curly black carpet. "Huh?"

Her eyes bulge a little in their sockets. She clasps her hands together, almost like she's praying. "Señorita Perez, you bring her back?"

I wonder just how much the maid knows. If, perhaps, Viviana confided in her . . . well, that might explain her standing stock still that day on the balcony, and giving me a good staring. But I don't have time to follow up all these loose threads, to track down every answer to put all the pieces of the puzzle together, I need to go save Viviana.

And so I say, "Can you tell me how I can get to Puente de los Duendes?"

CHAPTER THIRTY

Together, we go on back through the castle, and then down to the underground car park. Neither of us talking. And no one stops us to ask just where we're going, or what we're doing.

I dare to hope that Germo and the rest of the guards *are* out for the day.

At the same time, I hope against hope that I'm not too late.

That cement smell finally wafts over me as the doors to the lift slide open down at the underground car park. And I breathe in those scents of oil and spilled petrol. Of the stilted exhaust fumes that I guess will never quite escape from here.

I look over to the other side of the car park and see a pair of younger boys, about eighteen maybe, dressed up in light grey overalls and making good use of a power hose on a bright-red car.

I see, also, that the car has a flat tyre, and guess that they've been commandeered to fix it.

One of the boys nods to the other, and then, soon after, they're both looking over in our direction. Slight smirks on their lips. One of them wolf whistles.

I guess neither of them has seen the pistol I'm holding down at my side.

The maid waddles her way along with expert precision, apparently knowing just where she's going to. She heads up to a metal cabinet, an ugly light brown colour. Maybe the *only* ugly thing down here considering the rows and rows of sports cars.

Not to mention those sporty-looking motorbikes.

She dips into her skirt pocket again, withdraws that same, and apparently all-knowing, key card, and passes it over the scanner.

Another one of those satisfied *bleep-bleeps* and she peels the door open.

Inside I see the keys all nestled there.

"These cars of Señor Randolfo," she says.

I look over the keys. There are about ten hooks inside, and only two keys remaining. I look to the maid for guidance, but she just gives me a Gallic shrug in return.

I pluck out one of the keys, and then, showing just about all my pragmatic grace, I give the button a little squeeze.

Over on the other side of the car park, there's a loud *beep-beep*.

When I look over in the direction of the sound, I'm just in time to see the amber hazard lights blinking on the red sports car that the two boys in overalls are seeing to.

I notice that neither of them is smirking now.

And that, all of a sudden, they've got awfully occupied with their power hosing and cleaning.

I drop the key to the floor, and it lands with a *clatter* of metal. When I cast a sidelong glance to the maid, I catch her giving a wry smile. "Guess you're not Señor Randolfo's biggest fan?" I say.

I don't know whether she understands me completely, but she shakes her head with that same wry smile fixed on her lips, and I know that the words don't matter.

We understand one another *just fine*.

I pick off the last key there, give it a squeeze.

And—what do you know?—it belongs to one of the motorbikes parked up alongside us.

* * *

The motorbike is a sea-blue colour, and extremely shiny.

As I leap up onto the saddle, throw my leg over the other side, I feel the welt on my forehead give me a little prang. But I shove that sensation to the back of my mind. Because, now, I have to get my way to Viviana just as quickly as I possibly can.

See if there's *anything* I can do for her.

I fit the key into the ignition of the bike and then sit there. Just allowing myself to breathe deep for a little while. Ten seconds or so.

I look about me, past the maid waiting off on the periphery, still wide eyed and with her hands clasped down at her apron.

"No helmet?" I say, patting my head.

She shakes her head, and then points upwards, apparently indicating Randolfo's apartment.

Well, I guess I'm about to find out just where Spanish police stand on unhelmetted riders on their roads.

As I eye up the exit, I catch one of those boys glancing over in our direction, only for him to look away as quick as lightning, and to continue scrubbing away at that red sporty number, while his friend doesn't try to act as brave, and keeps himself ever busy with that power hose.

I look back to the maid, unable to stop a nervous, adrenaline-fueled smile breaking out on my lips. "What's your name?"

"Rosa," she says.

I hold out my hand.

She shakes it.

"Nice to meet you, Rosa." And then I look off to the exit of the underground car park, already visualising the road ahead. "I'll do my best to bring Viviana back, okay?"

She nods, smiles a little.

Then something strikes me.

I look round to her. "The front gate. How do I open the front gate?"

She just smiles back at me, points to the keys stuck in the ignition.

And that's when I see the little, dark green fob hanging off the key ring.

Guess I'm all set to go.

All ready to play the heroine.

CHAPTER THIRTY-ONE

The vibrations rumble up my spine. Bounce my bones about. I can feel the sun beaming down on the backs of my shoulders. Down onto my t-shirt. It's only when I'm about ten minutes out from the castle, hurtling down the slope from the castle—following Rosa's instructions—that I wonder if I should've brought a jumper with me.

Too late to turn back now, I guess.

As I pulled my way through the castle complex, and up to those gates, I managed to dig out a pair of sunglasses from inside one of the compartments. They're a bit masculine: that wrap-around, blackout variety, but they do a good job of keeping the wind out of my eyes . . . because a speck of dirt in the eye is all it would take for me to swerve off the road, break every bone in my body . . . and that's if I get lucky.

Because, if there's one thing I learned back on that motorbike course I took so many moons ago I have no intention of counting, it's that you never—*ever*—go riding without a helmet.

But I guess those rules never quite accounted for a situation like this.

Rules never do.

I have to concentrate on keeping my lips sealed, on actually pressing them tight together so I won't inhale the dusty air billowing up all around me. But I can still feel the one or two grains that have somehow snuck their way in.

Actually, I think that earthy taste is good for something.

It's good for purging the smell and taste of elderberries.

That's something that I hope I'll forget about soon.

I peer at the road ahead, check the signs.

This should be simple. Just a case of following the road. Looking out for the signs.

Rosa claimed that it was only forty-five minutes away.

But I'm determined to do it in less than twenty.

I guess if I'm going to get busted for riding without a helmet, I might as well go for a nice, fat speeding ticket too.

Not to mention the handgun shoved into the back of the waistband of my jeans.

* * *

The vibrations shake me right through to the roots of my teeth. But I don't mind. I know that I'm making great time on this. I'm really eating up the asphalt beneath me.

I don't care, either, about the panging, spine-numbing pain from the welt on my forehead, or that the wind against it might as well be a lashing whip.

I listen to the deafening *roar* of the engine, in high gear, and listen to the *crunch* of the dirt as it slips beneath my tyres.

Nothing else is on these roads. I know that it's off season but it seems vaguely ridiculous to me just how vacant of life this whole region is. I could probably count on one hand all the cars I've seen during my . . . well, I was about to say holiday, but I think *visit* might work a little better.

I glance up at the passing sign. Read off the white text on the blue background.

Puente de los Duendes.

Ten kilometres.

Looks like I *am* making record time after all.

As I follow the signs, I keep a good look out in my wing mirrors, at the road behind me, still unbelieving that I'll be able to make it all the way to the exchange point without some police car rolling up on my flanks.

But nothing.

All clear.

I glance up briefly at the arrow pointing off my turn, and then lean into it.

$$* * *$$

As I run down the gears, slowing a little, not wanting to give Randolfo and co a tipoff to my impending arrival, I reach back into the waistband of my jeans and bring out *Solecito*, hold it with my left hand, at the same time keeping my grasp tight on the handlebar grip.

I might need my quick draw here, else I might have some trouble.

Though, if these guys are all wandering about with semi-automatic rifles, I don't think it'll matter at all.

It's a big thing going up against a single rifle with a handgun, let alone *three* rifles.

But I shift those thoughts out of my brain and turn to examine the terrain.

That same pale orange dirt, I guess a relative of the dust that hangs around Brian's mansion. And there are boulders too.

I'm riding up a steady incline, and I know that, at any moment, it's going to plateau, and I'll need to be on my guard.

If I want to maintain the element of surprise.

As I sense the hill flattening out at the top of its summit, I gently ease off the accelerator, and then remove power completely. I allow the bike to drift over to the side of the road.

Its tyres crunch over the uneven dirt ground, and I bring the bike to a stop with a final, firm squeeze of the brakes, flip the kickstand, then switch off the ignition.

I listen as the engine ticks itself down, and only then realise just how badly my ears are ringing. I guess there are other reasons for wearing a helmet other than in case of falls.

I try to hear past that ringing sound in my ears, to hear anything that might alert me to my surroundings.

If my instinct is anything to go by, I'm guessing that I'm inside of a kilometre to Puente de los Duendes right now.

I breathe in hard. Try to keep my legs steady, because they keep wobbling about like jelly. I hold *Solecito* down at my thigh and slowly pick my way along the side of the road, staying just on the asphalt, just on the outside of the yellow lines.

As I go, my horizon is expanding. I can see more of the road up ahead.

I glance about, between the rolling yellow and green hills that surround the area, trying to get a glimpse at the bridge. But nothing. I can't see anything.

I pick my way on, still keeping to the asphalt, taking care not to send any pebbles skittering off into the dirt. Sending up a cloud of dust would be enough for a highly strung guard to catch sight of my location.

And to shoot.

Finally, the hill levels out.

I see the bridge stretched out before me.

A large flat patch of asphalt that stretches over a dried-up valley. Thick, steel-wound cables. A suspension bridge. At first I don't see the obvious, I'm so taken in by the bridge passing by just below the crest of the hill. And taking in just how large it is, and wondering about how I might've gone clear past without ever seeing it.

But then I do.

I catch sight of the car park, down on my left.

Germo's turtle-shell green van parked up there. And the other two matching ones.

A jet-black, scratched-up estate completes the line-up.

Then I see Randolfo, the two guards, Germo.

None of them have guns.

And then I see the face of the man meeting with Germo.

At first I can't believe it.

My heart swells in my throat.

My finger itches to squeeze the trigger.

It's the barman from *Por La Playa*.

CHAPTER THIRTY-TWO

stay right where I am. Afraid that if I shift from my spot they'll see me.

But I can hardly stand here forever either. I need to get moving. Have to get myself into the thick of the action.

Randolfo reaches forwards to shake the barman's hand, and I watch on as the barman gazes back over Randolfo's head.

I take in the barman's features again. That handlebar moustache. The shaved head. And those hazel eyes I can just make out from where I stand.

My heart beats against my throat. I know just what I need to do. That I have to fire off a shot, and right now. Because otherwise the barman will alert the others.

And the guards will scatter back to their vans.

But I can't.

Solecito remains stuck down at my side.

I feel the barrel against my thigh.

My mind tells me over and over again to take the shot, but instead I look back over the group gathered there, then to the barman's car, to the jet-black, scratched-up estate there.

No tinted windows.

I can see right into the backseat.

And that's where I see Viviana, gazing out at me, eyes wide, lips parted. But not making a sound. Sensible girl. She knows just what I've come for. That I'm here now to make everything all right again.

Just as I see the barman turn his head back to Randolfo, I finally break out of my daze.

Bring the pistol up.

Stare along the sight.

Aim at the barman's throat.

And fire.

✶ ✶ ✶

I see the blood spurt out of the barman's neck. Then the shot cracks out.

All around the valley.

As one, the two guards, along with Germo and Randolfo, all seem to drop to the ground.

Down into the pale orange dirt.

A cloud puffs up, and I see them all lying down there.

Hands over their heads.

But they have no guns.

I *remind* myself that they have no guns.

And that's when I see one of the guards reaching for his ankle.

I take aim. Fire again. Catch him in the shoulder.

He lets loose a groan of pain.

Blood spits out of him in a crimson dribble.

I see the other guard. Doing the same. Reaching for *his* ankle.

I take aim at him.

Fire too.

Catch him in just the same spot.

Another groan of pain.

Lots of writhing.

And I know that neither of these two will be able to keep their hands steady enough to take any sort of straight shot. Not today.

Germo and Randolfo have the good sense to stay totally still.

Hands still covering their heads as they lie facedown in the dust.

Guess they've got better survival instincts.

Or maybe their pay grade—their *rank*—allows them to sit out firefights.

And I remind myself of Germo, when he 'took care of' Señora Esmeralda.

That's the sort of man *he* is.

That's *his* sort of fight.

And I crunch my teeth together, feel my heart beating against my tonsils, and have to argue with myself not to shoot him dead right where he lies.

I turn my attention to the barman.

He slouches up against the side of his car.

Just over his shoulder, I can see Viviana nestled inside. Still motionless. And I wonder why she doesn't pull out her gun . . . the gun that surely *Daddy* has snuggled away somewhere on her person.

I could use a little help here rounding these boys up.

Five of them in all.

Three of them bleeding.

And two of them that I *want* to make bleed.

. . . If they'll only give me the chance.

I step along the asphalt. Keeping my eyes on them. *All* of them.

I guess they didn't expect any intervention.

Didn't expect Anna Harris to show up here.

Their formation shows that. The way they've boxed themselves in with their cars. Left themselves exposed to the higher ground.

They've got it all wrong.

As I draw closer, I feel a warm breeze blowing up behind me. Sending my hair bustling up a little. I can feel the dirt striking against my cheeks and, all of a sudden, I feel a fresh wave of pain through the welt on my forehead.

. . . As if the very act of drawing closer to Germo, the one that *gave* me this welt, causes it to flash with pain.

Maybe *I* should show him some pain.

But then my pragmatism kicks in once again. I remind myself that this *isn't* my country. That this isn't even *Brian's* country. And I have to take care.

No corpses.

None that can be traced to me, anyway . . .

I pick my way onto the rough, chewed-up dirt surface of the car park.

Germo and Randolfo both look up at me from their facedown positions, and I order them back to how they were.

They obey me.

You have no idea just how sweet *that* feels.

I look to the two guards.

Both breathing shallow breaths. Shoulders rising and falling. Blinking rapid-fire.

Good. Everything's good about that.

Sweat pooling on their foreheads and rolling down their cheeks in beads. Blood running out from their shoulders. Complexions pale.

But handguns still very much down at their ankles.

Strapped up out of sight.

That needs taking care of first up.

So, still keeping my other prisoners in sight, I stoop down, fish about at the legs of their suit trousers, feel the gun strapped to each guard, and then free each from its holster.

I pause a moment, and then toss each off into the distance. Into the dried-up thickets that surround us here. I listen to both guns land with a *crunch* of dirt, and see the light puff of dust.

That done, I turn my attention to Germo and Randolfo.

The two of them still cover their heads.

Keep their faces down in the dirt.

"All right," I say. "Get the hell up, both of you."

My pulse taps at the base of my tongue. A scream bounces about inside of my skull. But I stay calm on the outside. And keep myself aware of my surroundings.

Make sure I know what *each* and *every* one of these reprobates is doing.

Germo and Randolfo both get to their feet, instinctively keeping their hands on their heads. I wonder if they've been in a similar position before. If they've run into someone like me before.

They know the drill.

"Over there," I say, waggling the gun towards the bonnet of one of the turtle-shell green cars. It could be Germo's, or one of the two guard's. I don't care to tell them apart any longer.

Germo and Randolfo do as they're told, continuing to face me.

I watch them all the way over to the bonnet, and then turn to the guards. Issue them the exact same order. They follow the good example set by their bosses very nicely indeed, and just like that I have four men all lined up on one of the bonnets of the turtle-shell green vans.

Keeping them in sight, right before me, I take a couple of steps back, back towards the barman.

I see that he's breathing hard too. Just like the two guards. But, when I risk a quick glance down, I see that I only caught the fleshy part of his throat. He'll scar, but he'll live.

At least that's my inexpert opinion.

Still keeping myself facing Randolfo, the guards, and, of course, Germo, I make sure my voice is firm, uncompromising, as I address the barman. "Keys," I say.

There's a slight *jangle*. I don't dare look back at him.

"Open it," I say.

I hear his heavy breathing. "Is not . . ." he says, sounding strained, "is not . . ."

This time I do risk a glance back at him. See that he's offering up the keys to me. And I realise that it's an old-style key.

Not one of these with a remote control fob.

I guess I had to run into *some* trouble today.

But I handle it just fine, reaching back, taking the keys off him.

And then, keeping my eyes stuck on Randolfo, the guards and Germo, I feel for the hole in the door, then slip the key in with a grating sound.

I feel the weight of the aged mechanism as I turn the key. The *snick* of the locks all popping off at the same time.

The back door opens with an unoiled *creak*, and I know, without looking around, that Viviana has got herself free.

I can hardly keep myself from giving a wry smile before I hear the *click* of her priming the pistol as she says, "Drop the gun."

CHAPTER THIRTY-THREE

All **at once** it feels like I've just plunged underwater. A freezing cold sensation rolls over my skin. Brings all my hairs to a standing position. I keep *Solecito* firm in my grasp.

"I will not ask another time," she says.

And she sounds like she means it.

I look out ahead of me, to Germo, and to Randolfo. They still have their hands on their heads, but I can see that there's the trace of a smirk there. Growing on each of their lips.

I run a quick calculation in my brain. Think about whether or not I can get away with popping one of them with a bullet.

If I only have the chance to take out one, I know who it'll be.

And no prizes for guessing either.

"Throw the gun!" she says, this time shriller.

Though I'm sure it's impossible, just my imagination, I'm certain I can hear the gentle *creak* of her finger depressing the trigger, just a little more.

I stare up, into the sky. The deep-blue sky. And then I let loose a little sigh.

I throw *Solecito*.

It lands about ten paces away.

A slight *crunch*. A little puff of dust. Just like the two guards' guns.

"Hands on your head!"

I do what she asks.

Down at my feet, I can hear the suckle of the barman's breathing. Know that, though I haven't hit anything that important, he's most likely in a lot of pain. Maybe on the brink of passing out. Probably needs medical attention.

But maybe he should've thought about people like me before he got into this business of buying up pretty girls in lieu of debts.

"On your knees!"

Again, I do just what she says.

I feel the grit and heavier stones through the fabric of my jeans.

As the sun beats down on me, I feel a hard throb through my forehead, from where Germo hit me. And it angers me that now he'll get another chance.

Another chance to dispose of me.

I watch the guards, Germo and Randolfo, all four of them, bring their hands off their heads. Wander away from the spot I got them all lined up so nicely.

I want to screw my eyes up, pummel my fists against the ground.

With a nod from Randolfo, the two guards make off into the dried-up thickets, where I tossed their guns, apparently to go and look for them.

Now—*right* now—I regret not having come up with a more lasting solution.

Still, though, I guess it'll take them a good few minutes of scrounging around.

And that might be all I need.

I listen in to the twin *crunches* of shoes over dirt as Viviana moves closer to me. Though I don't dare look back, I try to imagine, to map out in my mind, her position.

And I guess that she's about seven, maybe eight paces behind.

Not yet.

I can't risk it yet.

I observe Germo head back for his van. And I dread what's about to happen. But, at the same time, I know there's nothing I can do to stop it.

Not unless the stars align.

Not unless . . .

Another few crunches.

I can hear Viviana's breathing. Can almost feel the warmth from her body. I'm certain that a waft of peach perfume passes over me.

I keep facing forwards. Watch Germo open up the driver's door of his van. Bend inside. Reach across to the glove compartment on the passenger's side.

It's now or never.

Life or death.

Does it really matter any more?

∗ ∗ ∗

I suck in my cheeks and, in a swift movement, swing myself back, ducking at the same time.

Viviana fires the gun.

The bullet zips by my ear.

And my eardrums descend into a throbbing ringing sound.

But I keep my wits about me.

See her there. Grasping the pistol in both hands. Eyes wide. Muscles all stiff. Lips parted.

Just a frightened little girl.

That's all.

I grab hold of her forearm.

She fires the gun again.

Into the dust again.

I bring my hand down onto her arm in a chop, and with my other hand seize hold of the grip of the pistol. All at once, I feel her muscles slacken. Give up the struggle.

And now *I* have the gun.

Before she gets her wits together, I give her a smack on the forehead with the butt of the pistol. I watch her eyes swivel upwards in their sockets. And she crumples to the ground.

Lands just beside the barman.

I spin around.

Catch sight of Germo on the way out.

Nostrils flared.

Alarmed.

And with a pistol of his own in his hand.

Now I guess we get to see just who's *really* the best.

Perhaps the best thing I can say about Germo is that he's fearless. A competitor. Pure and simple. He waits no time at all before firing off a shot from behind the relative safety of the opened front door of his van.

Over my shoulder, glass tinkles as the bullet shatters one of the side windows of the barman's car.

My turn.

I take a shot.

Not a good one.

The bullet catches the door of his car. Dents it. That's all.

Maybe I hadn't accounted for bulletproof vans.

But what did I expect?

His turn.

He fires again.

This time the bullet skips the hair of my forearm.

Behind me there's a narrow, and snakelike *hiss*.

One of the tyres of the barman's car being punctured.

All the air being let out.

I take aim again.

Hit the glass of the door he stands behind.

A spider web-like pattern splits the glass.

No tinkle.

What do you know?

. . . Bulletproof glass too.

Off in the distance, I'm half aware of Randolfo, and of the two guards. But I can't allow myself to look away. If I look away, it might well be the very last thing I do.

First Germo. Then the rest. Like dominos.

Germo brings his gun out over the top of the door. Fires off four or five shots. I lose count. Just about the worst thing that can happen in a gunfight.

I won't know when he'll need to reload.

He must be close though.

All his shots miss.

They pummel the car behind me.

More breaking glass. Warping bodywork. Hisses of air leaving tyres.

On that very last shot he gets sloppy.

And I see right through it.

Take *advantage* of it.

He leaves his gun hand exposed. At the top of the car door.

I take aim. Fire.

He lets out a yelp of pain, like a dog kicked by its owner.

He ducks down out of sight.

Leaves a bloody smear on the cracked glass of the driver's door.

I take my opportunity to read my surroundings.

Randolfo, I see, is running.

Running away from here.

At full sprint.

Already a good fifty, maybe sixty, feet away from us.

I glance back to Germo, and decide to take a chance.

I line up the shot. Focus on Randolfo's back. And fire.

The shot cracks out. Echoes all around me. Numbs my eardrums a little more.

But Randolfo drops.

. . . Like a sack of potatoes, as I believe the expression goes.

Next to the guards, both of them have abandoned their search. Their eyes are focussed on me. And, a second or so later, white-faced from their injuries, they both have their hands up in the air again.

Guess I did better with my throw than I thought.

I allow myself the briefest of smirks. Then remind myself that the battle's not over yet.

Not by a longshot.

I turn my attention back to Germo.

Can *hear* him squirming about behind the driver's door of his car.

Now's the time for the final move.

And it looks like it'll be me who makes it.

I creep my way along the dirt. Feeling it crunch and crumble beneath my trainers. And I draw closer.

And closer.

Heart beating hard against my ribs.

Before I know it, I'm there. Standing over him.

His right hand is a mess.

And his blood is crimson in the sunlight.

His gun useless, discarded beside him in the dirt.

And his eyes roll up at me.

Pleading for mercy.

I reach out with my foot, bring his gun under the sole of my trainers. Scoot it back, far away from where he can grab it in a hurry.

Then I bring my own gun down to my thigh.

My hand shakes.

I remember my Kill Switch is busted.

I allow myself a well-earned breath of air and say, "This time. Just this one time."

CHAPTER THIRTY-FOUR

Funny how everything seems to move much faster—more efficiently—whenever I'm in charge.

First things first, I work on bringing everyone in again. The two guards, *both* of them still bleeding, work to carry their boss, Randolfo, back towards the car park.

Meanwhile, I help Germo to his feet, and then get him all seated back in his van.

I do a quick search of the van's interior to make sure there aren't any other guns knocking about, and it seems to be clean. The other two vans too.

I guess even Randolfo, a man of *his* apparent standing, didn't want to get himself caught packing some semi-automatic rifles.

Next I turn my attention to Viviana, still knocked out, and the barman who's still slumped up against his car—eyes lolling about their sockets but still on the brink of consciousness.

I decide that I'm going to have to be the one to take pity on the barman. Though, by all rights, I should simply finish him off.

Whatever business he's involved with—whatever people he works for—I know just what they represent, and it sickens me, that they would *allow* something like this.

One thing, though, still sits badly with me. And it's the reason just why Viviana decided to turn that gun onto me.

Was it some mistaken sense of loyalty?

Didn't she say something about how she'd never be able to shirk the love of her father . . . whatever that was supposed to mean.

Maybe that was it.

Maybe I can work *that* out later on.

I grab a hold of the barman's hand, help him back onto his feet.

Today he's wearing a light-green shirt, and it's already gone a pretty unsightly purplish colour from all the blood he's been losing.

With my free hand, just about supporting him against my other shoulder, I open up the back door of the car, and then get him sat down on the seat, doing my best not to plump him down on too much glass as I go . . . but in any case, figuring that, most likely, it'll be safety glass anyway, I let him go.

And does he really *not* deserve just a few fragments of glass up his backside?

As I settle him down on the backseat, I begin to turn my mind to practicalities, to how I'm going to extricate myself from this particular spot.

Well, I still have the motorbike tucked away at the roadside . . . though I don't suppose riding without a helmet after having taken part in a gun battle is the best way *not* to attract attention from the police.

Then I look back over the vans: those three, turtle-shell green vans, for all intents and purposes identical. Oh sure, Germo's van got pretty shot up in our little melee, but the other two are fine.

Spotless, actually, apart from a few lashings of dust here and there.

Nothing to give them away as being vans involved in a shoot-out, in any case.

Looking at the four of them: Germo, Randolfo and the two guards, I have an inkling that only one of them is going to be in any sort of state for driving.

Maybe none of them.

And I certainly wouldn't count on either Viviana or the barman being in any fit state to drive either . . . because I am supposing they're all going to be driving off together.

So they'll only need *one* of those vans at all.

Perhaps it's time to make Randolfo a deal he—literally—can't refuse.

Just as I'm on the brink of heading off, of petitioning Randolfo for the keys of one of his extremely fetching vans, the barman makes a gurgling sound from over my shoulder.

I turn and look to him.

He squeezes his eyes shut, and then opens them wide. I can see the webbing of red veins sprouting all about his eyeballs. "Ah . . . ah . . ."

I glance back to Randolfo and the other three, then down to Viviana, making sure that he's not giving me some sort of a warning.

Nope.

Viviana's still all knocked out.

Randolfo and co pretty much incapacitated too.

And so I cock my head back in his direction.

"Ah . . . ah," he tries again, and then he finally seems to get his throat clear, to get out just what he wants to say this time. "Bry-*un*."

My heart squeezes in my chest. Blood rushes through my veins. That throbbing on my right temple beats a little harder. "What?" I say. "What was that?"

The barman manages a slight smile beneath that handlebar moustache of his, and I know that he's got the message through that he wanted.

Now it's my turn to deal with it.

Brian?

How does he know about Brian?

As I look over him, I see his lips breaking out into a smile, a *wide* smile. And that smile tells me all that I need to know. That Brian is behind all this.

That the barman *works* for Brian.

∗ ∗ ∗

At least that gets the lifts sorted, if nothing else.

I guess, the way that things have played out, I'm going to be riding with the barman. Taking him off to hospital.

When I finally approach Randolfo, meet those jittery eyes of his, and watch those winces of pain as he bleeds the blood out of his back from where I shot him, he seems perfectly happy about me commandeering one of his vans.

In fact he makes no comment about me having to return it ever.

So maybe I'll get to keep it after all.

Thinking about it, I'm not really much of a fan of the colour.

But it'll get me back to the mansion—to *Brian's* mansion—if nothing else.

And so I help the barman into the backseat of the van, keys in my other hand, and then shut him up inside.

I look back over Randolfo, give him my best salute . . . he only gives a faint groan back . . . and then I look to Viviana, still knocked out, poor girl, but I guess that she'll be perfectly capable of driving them back to the Castillo de los Llanos later on—I mean when she wakes up.

I stoop down and retrieve *Solecito* from where I tossed it, and then, with both Viviana's gun and my own, I turn my attention to our getaway car.

I slot myself into the driver's seat of the van, turn the ignition, feel the wonderful, *fresh* blow of the air conditioning in my sweat-soaked hair, and then I pull us out of the car park, crunching our way out across the dirt.

For the first time since I ran into Randolfo, had the *misfortune* of striking up an acquaintance with him, I think that I've finally got myself shot of that taste of elderberries in my mouth.

∗ ∗ ∗

While we drive, I look out for any signs of hospitals, because I guess that's the best place for me to take the barman now. At least, *I* don't have much of an idea of how I might go patching him up.

I glance back into the backseat a few times, keeping an eye on him, not quite trusting the odd snatched glance in the rear-view mirror. As I drive on, watching the asphalt sweep beneath the van, the broken yellow lines working at hypnotising me, I think back over the barman's role in that whole exchange. Wonder whether I was right to shoot him.

He was about to reveal my location.

Or was he?

Was it simply my jumpy trigger finger coming to bear on proceedings?

I look back at him, see that contorted face of his, and then catch sight of a large, blocky white-lettered capital 'H' up on the blue sign at the side of the road.

That's where we need to head, or that's what I think as I tilt the wheel, before the barman breaks into his blabbering again. He's not speaking Spanish *or* English. Just sounds.

But that shaking of the head is pretty distinctive and, I think, tells me just about everything I need to know.

When I look him over again, I see that his complexion is a little fuller now. And that he's torn off the sleeve of his shirt and is using it to apply pressure to the neck wound.

I shrug my shoulders. "Where to then?"

He draws a few hard breaths then says, ". . . The man-*shun.*"

I straighten the van back up, and proceed along the road, seeing a signpost for San Floriano that I'm sure will steer me back in the right direction, back towards Brian's mansion.

* * *

Twilight is already sweeping in as I watch the steady glow of the van's headlights up ahead of us. It's incredible how much the headlights cut into the darkness, even in comparison to Box Wagon they're bright and all-encompassing.

I fear for any native, nocturnal wildlife here.

I guess it'll never look at the place the same way again.

If it sees at all after being blinded by *these* lights.

My heart ticks along slower now. My mouth is dry, and tastes stale. I can feel more than a little dirt sticking to my skin.

I reach out and press the button to wind down the driver's window.

Fresh air blows in through the narrow crack.

Fresh *sea* air.

I breathe in its thickness, feeling my tongue grow slick over that salty edge to it.

In fact, I get so absorbed by it, and the idea of those lapping crystal waves that I almost miss the turning off the main road, the one that leads onto the dirt track to Brian's mansion.

Maybe I had half an idea of leaving the barman back at *Por La Playa*, or maybe I just wasn't thinking at all.

For the *first* time this holiday.

We rumble our way along the dirt path and, as we pass by that steep slope, I can't help but stare off into the darkness, into the valley down there.

But I see nothing.

Nothing at all.

Has Randolfo already had his men come by to take care of Señora Esmeralda, and her canary-yellow car?

I make a note to myself to come out here in the morning and make sure.

A long-buried anger stirs within me again, and I think about how it's been over a month since I was in the mansion here. Since I was *taken* away from here.

I sweep up to the mansion, that great white monolith, and I pause before reminding myself that this van I'm driving most likely won't fit in the garage.

Next thing I realise is that Box Wagon's not out here where I left it . . . where Germo and his two cronies dragged me out of it.

Someone—Germo?—must've parked it back inside. Shut up the place. Makes sense.

Better not to leave a mansion like this, all the way out here in the middle of nowhere, totally unguarded.

No way of knowing what sort of people might be bobbing about.

And so I park up the van, switch off the ignition and then leap down out of the driver's seat. I help the barman out from the back and, together, we hobble our way up the stone steps to the door of the mansion.

And it's then that I realise I don't have keys.

I look to the barman, for some reason out of expectation.

He grins back at me, still holding that scrap of shirt to his throat, and then he raps his knuckles against those hefty, oak monstrosities.

A pause.

Shuffle of footsteps inside.

The door opens a crack.

And—what do you know?—it's Brian.

Brian Mathewson.

CHAPTER THIRTY-FIVE

For a second, the sea breeze gets the better of me, that pure salty taste seeming to strip the words right off my tongue. And I get a fresh waft of that cinnamon scent of floor cleaner that Señora Esmeralda applied to the marble floor of the front hall on the last day of her life.

Then the welt on my right temple, where Germo punched my lights out, tingles and feels sharp all of a sudden. And then all the croaking bugs come back to me, as if in a single, solid wave.

My eyes find Brian's.

He gives me one of his smuggest of grins. "Do come in, old girl, would hate to leave you out here on the doorstep."

Then he shifts his attention to the barman, and he says something in Spanish, the barman gives a slight grin, and brings the scrap of material away from his throat so that Brian can see the wound there.

Brian looks back at me. "Goodness," he says. "I can see that you've been making friends in your usual way."

I feel frozen. Like all the blood in my veins has just frozen solid. My muscles, too, feel like they can't move at all, except to hold rigid so that I can keep on supporting the barman at my side.

Brian calls back into the mansion, and then, dressed in a dressing gown, I now realise, one of the white fluffy ones that I tottered about the mansion in, he takes the load of the barman off me, and together the two of them stagger in through the front hall, and through to the kitchen.

With nothing else to do, no one to tell me *what* to do, I simply bring the large oak doors shut behind me with a *slap*, and then I wander my way upstairs.

* * *

I go up to the master bedroom first, probably because I want to throw myself down on a bed, sleep for a solid twelve hours. But, when I get up there, stand in the doorway, I realise that it's stuffed with Brian's things.

My brain just about catches up with me then, and I remember that this is Brian's house after all, and now that he's arrived he's perfectly entitled to take the master bedroom.

Even *I* can't begrudge him that.

So I pick out another of the bedrooms, lie down for a while, but find it impossible to sleep. Though the sheets are silk, just like the master bedroom, as soft as I could want, I just can't get myself comfortable.

When I open the window wide I feel a little better. The sea breeze wafting in over me. That salty, yet *fresh* sensation coming inside.

I reach up to my temple, feel the welt bulky beneath my fingers, and I wonder if I should do something about it.

When I go through into the en suite, take a look, I see that it's all purple, a kind of golden green about the edges. I run a little cold water and dab at it with my fingers.

It feels good.

A little soothing.

Then I eye the shower cubicle and get a better idea.

∗ ∗ ∗

All washed and clean, I pluck one of those fluffy white dressing gowns out of the wardrobe, shrug it about my shoulders, and then pad my way—*barefooted*—down the stairs, and back into the front hall.

It turns out that I'm just in time to see Brian and a man I haven't seen before, a man carrying a neat, bulging satchel, heading for the front doors.

Brian stops dead, looks over at me, that same infuriating smile pressing back his cheeks. "Anna," he says, far too brightly for my liking, "I'm just showing the doctor out. Do go on into the kitchen, I've cooked up something. Sure you'll feel better once you've got it all packed away in your belly."

I linger a moment, look to the doctor's face, give him a pleasant smile, and then drag myself off to the kitchen.

∗ ∗ ∗

Right now, the whole kitchen stinks of disinfectant, and I see, from the bloodied white cloth that lies over the marble-surfaced kitchen table, that this has become the impromptu surgery.

I guess that Brian's had the barman taken off some place so that he can get a rest.

To one of the many expansive bedrooms upstairs.

I find the food that Brian's left out for me. All in a saucepan, and just ready to be heated up for my consumption. When I peer inside, I see that it's paella.

That makes me wonder, wonder if this is Señora Esmeralda's paella, perhaps one that she left in the freezer for Brian . . . did she know that he was on his way out here? . . . Had he tipped her off?

I think back to the phone call, and the timing of Señora Esmeralda's visit.

Would there be any other reason for her turning up for work on a Sunday?

Guess I won't know till I ask.

I flip the heat on under the saucepan, wait a grand total of maybe two minutes before I dish the paella all out—steaming—onto a porcelain plate.

I decide not to set myself up at the kitchen table, some nagging gut feeling reminding me that blood and food aren't always the best of mixes.

So I hoik myself off to the sitting room, flick on the nuclear TV, and then let random Spanish television wash over me, and I allow myself to become hypnotised in its crazy, multi-coloured dance.

A little while later, me propped up on the white leather sofa, about three quarters of the way through decimating my paella, I hear Brian's steady footsteps. Hear his heavy breathing just behind me. I don't need to turn around to know that he's there.

I feel him linger in the doorway. Never really come inside.

He says nothing, and I say nothing back.

When I finish up the paella, that wonderful, oily, rich taste of fish filling all of my senses, I do look back to Brian, still standing over there in the doorway.

He has his hands in the pockets of his white fluffy dressing gown, and though he's looking at the television screen, I can see that he's really using it as an excuse to stare into space. To blank his mind totally.

All of a sudden, he seems to realise that I'm watching. And he puts on that familiar smile of his. He clears his throat, and then says, "We'll talk about everything tomorrow, Anna, okay?" before he sweeps on out of the sitting room.

That just leaves me alone with the TV.

All the actors in this soap opera speaking in a language that I don't understand.

CHAPTER THIRTY-SIX

Maybe I expect to sleep for hours and hours—no doubt that my muscles, my *mind*, are all demanding that I do. But, in the end, I wake up with the rising sun.

See that grapefruit coloured light brightening the horizon. And, a little beyond, the bluish, marble-like glow of the sea. I determine that that's where we're headed. Me and Brian. Today.

Later on, when Brian gets up and gets himself dressed, we head down to the garage, pick up the Box Wagon. This time, he drives . . . something I'm not all that bothered about, all told, and we take the right onto the asphalt road and head for the beach.

Though Brian has the air conditioners flushing out freezing cold air, I zap my window down with the button at my elbow, and feel the sea breeze blow into the car.

The smell just revitalises me. Brings me back to life. Even despite the fairly sleep-light night.

I can still taste the warm embrace of that thick, hearty hot chocolate

Brian boiled the two of us up this morning. And I can't help feeling positive about the day ahead . . . about my *life* ahead now that Brian is here.

Though there are certainly some things to be swept beneath the carpet. That's for certain.

First thing I notice, as Brian slows Box Wagon, brings us down the cobblestoned hill and into San Floriano, is that the brightly coloured houses, with all their turquoises, those pinks, those yellows, all have their shutters cast off. That chipboard that used to cover the windows and doors all torn away.

The change is so startling for me that, on instinct, I look over at Brian, who merely grips on tight to the steering wheel, continues to trace the road ahead. He smiles slightly. "Guess this all looks quite different with a few people pottering about, eh?"

I turn back to look out from under the windscreen, out to the families that stream back and forth along the promenade in the beaming sunshine, frolicking down on the pale-blue pebbled beach, and I can't help but think that he's right.

∗ ∗ ∗

Once Brian's parked up Box Wagon, we head straight for the beach bar, without any sort of discussion between the two of us.

I look up to the weathered chunk of wood, to the white-painted letters up there, spelling out the name of the bar.

Por La Playa.

I take in the roof of dried rushes, and the wooden-topped stools all cemented to the ground, and drawn up to the dark wood counter.

Today all the stools are occupied.

Kids. Mothers. Fathers. Grandmothers. Grandfathers.

Some have ice creams in their hands. Clutched in their fists. They lick at them as they melt down the cone.

Others, the parents, the grandparents, have a drink set before them. A perspiring glass. With variously coloured straws with neat, obtuse angles bent into them.

I look over them, though, look past them. And I see the barman standing there.

It's only then that I think to turn into Brian, and ask, "What's his name?"

The skin about Brian's eyes creases up in amusement. "You really are a friendly, old soul, aren't you?"

"Just tell me."

"Hugo," he says, making it sound more like 'Oo-go.'

Guess that's the proper pronunciation.

I try it out a couple of times, and then stride up to the bar, Brian tottering alongside me.

Hugo has gauze stuck onto his neck from where I shot him, but other than that he seems to be in high spirits. *Much* higher sprits than whenever he served me alone here, in any case.

That might be due for a change now that I've shown up.

But, against my judgement, he catches Brian's eye, and then mine. And he smiles at the both of us fully, his handlebar moustache seeming like the perfect inversion of his grin.

He finishes up serving an elderly lady with grey hair, and wearing a pair of lilac shorts, and then he shifts off along his bar, pours out a couple of drinks then lays them down on the counter. With a grin, he says, "On the house," before moving away from us, going back to serving the customers there.

Brian takes hold of his drink, which I see is whisky with about twice the serving of ice he usually has . . . I suppose he needs something to see off this overly warm weather.

Mine is the lime juice and fizzy water.

What can I say? I guess that, by now, Hugo knows what his regulars order.

With our drinks in hand, me and Brian head for the promenade. And we lean up against the rusted-up metal banister looking out to sea. Over the beach with all its merry blues and reds, and yellows, all the joy of a family day out.

Both of us stare out to sea and, after a couple of minutes, with the sun beating down on my bare head, warming up my brain, turning it to mush, I find myself finally zoning out. Getting myself to relax for really the first time in my holiday.

And that's when Brian says, "Well, I guess that I owe you something of an explanation."

I raise a smirk to that. "It'd be nice of you."

He lets out a heavy sigh, his shoulders rising and falling as he does so. "Right then, I think it can be summed up quite neatly, without too much of a scrap of doubt."

"I'm looking forward to it."

He smiles gently. "First of all, when I received that call from you—the day back at the mansion, when you told me about Señora Esmeralda, well, that just got right to me. Jabbed me right in the gut. She was a wonderful lady: kind, honest, and caring with everything to do with keeping the mansion in top nick."

I think about Señora Esmeralda, and our micro battles, and I wonder if I see her in a different light now that she's gone forever.

I should, shouldn't I?

Brian continues, "So, I had my people look into it, and—"

"I thought you said I had to take care with Randolfo, and I got the impression that you were afraid of him in some way . . . just how it came across on the phone."

Brian sips at his whisky, now almost totally iced water, and then says, "Absolutely, which is why I got in touch with Hugo here, asked him whether he might be able to look into things here. To find out just what it was that Randolfo's been up to . . . why he's been bothering my golden girl."

I smirk at that comment, but deep down I feel it warming me, and it makes me glad. I turn my mind back to what Brian's saying, flash a look back to the bar, and catch those immersive hazel eyes of Hugo's.

Hugo gives me a smile.

I turn back to Brian. "I had no idea that Hugo would be wrapped up so tight in all that sort of thing."

Brian rolls his eyes as if he's insinuating I'm some sort of dunce. "Oh, come on, Anna. A man running a beach bar all the year round, most of the time to an empty beach, and you *really* believe that the man's on the level?"

"Yes," I try, my voice going all reedy.

Brian slurps up the last of his iced water / whisky, and then dangles his emptied glass by the tips of his fingers. "No, Hugo is well connected all right, and he managed to get right through to the very crux of what Randolfo was up to and, with my money, managed to buy himself into a position of great power."

"And what's that?" I say, realising that I might as well let Brian treat me like a bimbo . . . if it means he's just going to feed me the whole story straight.

Brian fixes me with a gaze, but falls short of looking all disapproving and parental this time. "He managed to buy off the debt, and get himself into the position of the exchange for Viviana, to be the one to take her off her father's hands."

"But Randolfo planned for Viviana to kill the person who picked her up."

Brian flashes his eyebrows. "And how was I supposed to know that?" he says, sounding like I've touched a slight nerve. "I mean, that's the reason that Hugo does these sorts of things—trust me, he is paid very well."

"And what would Hugo have done with Viviana after? . . . I mean, supposing that Viviana didn't shoot and kill him?"

"Well, the idea was simply for Hugo to get Viviana as far away from her father as possible and then to set her free. That was the full extent of the plan."

"That sounds awfully noble, coming from you."

Brian grins, flushes slightly. "Let's just say that we never reached the showdown, so there's really no need to talk about it."

"You were thinking of using Viviana in some sort of bargain with Randolfo, weren't you? To try and leverage a little more power, to make him feel a little less . . ."

Brian holds up his hand for me to stop. "Really, my dear, you'll get nothing at all out of me. Don't think that one acquires power by spelling out every last detail of one's plans."

I guess he's got a point there, however *annoying* it truly is.

"What about Viviana, why did she stop me from rescuing her?"

Brian shrugs. "Family honour. She probably had her father's plan at heart. Thought that she was doing a favour."

"Then maybe it would've been better if I'd just left things alone—allowed them to play out?"

"Well, that might've mean Hugo snuffing it, I mean, if you *really* taught Viviana everything you know."

My stomach dips. I know he's right. Now I suddenly feel a little better about having stepped in. Almost everything has come out fine. And, for once, despite how little I *truly* knew about what was going on, it seems like I haven't made any great mistakes.

But there is something that still hangs over me like a brimming storm cloud.

I look out to sea, suck in another dose of that salty air, and then say, "And what happens to Germo, to the man who *killed* Señora Esmeralda?"

Brian snorts a laugh as if this is just about the most amusing thing he's ever heard. As if just *thinking* about the thing amuses him. Still staring out to sea, clasping the rail, he says, "Gun still in that van you arrived in last night?"

"Yes," I say, and then, "why?"

"I think I've got a plan for our friend Germo."

"And what's that?"

Brian shrugs. "Police."

"But my prints are on it—"

Brian taps the bridge of his nose, then winks for good measure.

I look back out to sea, my vision going all blurry with the sparkling water.

We stand there, leaning on the rail, for another good few minutes before Brian turns sidelong, gives *another* of his sighs, and then says, "So, have you come to any conclusion as to the future of your career. As to your future with Mathewson Media?"

✳ ✳ ✳

I know that the question has been coming. That it's been lurking as a subtext for the whole of the conversation. For the whole of the *holiday*. But now, now that it's out in the open, I can't help but feel those chilling prickles dancing out all over my skin. And shadows of all those nightmares drifting back through my mind.

What's my answer?

. . . I haven't killed anyone, not for a while, anyway.

I *could* have killed Germo, I guess, I wouldn't have had a *problem* doing it. But I held back.

Is that all it takes?

Was my conscience clear while I fought with him, prepared to *kill* him?

Maybe my Kill Switch is all right now. Maybe I've got it back. Maybe I can simply flush everything else from my mind. Make clean kills.

I guess there will only ever be one way of knowing.

One way to find out.

Because, one thing's for certain, though I might have a cool half a million pounds in the bank, that's not going to be enough for me to escape.

To *disappear*.

Forever.

. . . Or could I just go through a career change? Do something else entirely?

A teacher . . . a plumber . . . a gardener . . .

But I would still have the killing instinct inside of me, and who would be able to tell just when it would come out?

Because *I* certainly can't control it.

Does working for Brian, taking care of people, is that some way for me to channel something that's totally natural, almost completely uninhibited?

Or is it just an excuse?

Brian slips me another of his sidelong smiles, then he gives a yawn, a stretch, and he brings his hand down on my shoulder. "No rush, old girl, really. Think it over a little while more. I mean, it's not like you've had much of a holiday out here, is it?"

I raise an empty smile to his. "No," I say, "I suppose not."

He steers us off back towards *Por La Playa*, and I get the impression that Brian's just getting started on his drinking. That this is very much the early rounds for him.

"Thinking about going to a bullfight," he says. "Tomorrow afternoon, maybe, if you'd like to join me."

"Sounds horrible," I say.

He gives me a smirk, then continues to guide me through the crowds of smiling families, and back to the counter of the bar. As he stands there, elbow resting on the counter, he meets my eye, his smirk fades a little, and I notice the slight hardness that enters his eye. "You know, Anna, the one problem you have?"

"No? What's that?"

"You take life *far* too seriously. Never let your hair down. Have some fun."

I turn myself around, prop my own elbows onto the bar counter, and stare back out to sea. "Yeah," I say, "you're probably right."

Because all that's on my mind, despite the stretched out bluish horizon, the apparently endless sparkling sea, all that's in my mouth, is blood.

Crimson. Thick. Sticky.

And on my hands.

THE END

AUTHOR'S NOTE

Just a quick message to thank you so much for taking the time to read one of my stories.

It would be wonderful if you could take a moment to leave a review on the sales page for this title. These help an enormous amount in finding more readers who might enjoy the book!

If you want to hear about my latest releases, and pick up some email-exclusive bonuses, you can sign up here: www.aviain.com/readers

Thanks for reading!

AV Iain

ABOUT THE AUTHOR

AV Iain:

Crime, suspense and mystery. A dash of horror at times.

His main series features snarky female assassin Anna Harris. Like most mothers, she strives to strike the ever-elusive balance between her personal and professional life. And mostly fails.

Will she ever be able to get it together, or will it all simply fall apart?

For email-exclusive bonuses, news of latest releases, and more, you can sign up for AV Iain's newsletter here: www.aviain.com/readers

COMPLIMENTARY
DIGITAL EDITION

A complimentary digital edition is
included with this book.

To download your epub, mobi
& PDF versions of this book, please navigate to
www.dibbooks.com/digital-editions/ and when
prompted for a password enter the following:

bullfighting